SEAN

YEAGER

and the DNA Thief

D. M. JARRETT

For more information about Sean Yeager
Adventures visit: **www.SeanYeager.com**

Sean Yeager returns in:
Hunters Hunted
Claws of Time
Mortal Thread

SEAN YEAGER

and the DNA Thief

Sean Yeager is a determined teenager drawn into an ancient
and perilous struggle. Following an unexplained burglary,
Sean's life is turned upside down when he discovers enemies
and abilities he never knew he had. He is protected by a
mysterious organisation called the Foundation, but can they
be trusted, and are they as formidable as they appear? Sean
tries to recover his most prized possessions and searches for
clues about his missing father, if he can survive long enough.

UK enhanced third edition

This edition published by XLT Consulting Ltd.
www.SeanYeager.com

This edition first published in 2019.
First published in 2012.

A CIP catalogue record for this book is available from the British Library.

ISBN 978-0-9573751-2-3

For adventurers young and old.

With grateful thanks and appreciation to Sean, Mary, and Freddie.

.

CONTENTS

CHAPTER 1: ALERT

It was a bright, sunny day. Between showers, it was refreshing and warm. Beneath them, it was like being assaulted by a power-washer. Steam rose from the pavements, and passers-by hurried between rain shelters. Meanwhile, sinister clouds loomed overhead. Another deluge was due at any moment.

Sean Yeager and his mother, Sarah, arrived home after a tedious shopping trip. The regular stores had sold out of grey school trousers, and Sean was elated at the prospect of being unable to return to school. Mrs Yeager, however, was less than impressed, grumpy even. She glanced in the rear-view mirror, threw back her long blonde hair and let out a silent scream. Her day had unravelled into a mess, and her roots were in dire need of attention. As for her wardrobe, she was still making do with last year's clothes, which were now threadbare. She consoled herself that at least she had managed to regain her trim figure, thanks to her park runs and the slimming club. But what about Sean's school uniform? Where on Earth would they find three pairs of grey trousers in only two days?

Mrs Yeager alighted on the driveway outside their house. It was a humble, red brick dwelling in a small town, but it was home. Car doors clunked, and keys rattled in the front door to sighs of relief all round. A 'welcome' doormat invited them in to a faint smell of baking and fingerprint-marked wallpaper. All that was missing was a dog. They were forbidden according to a shambolic man from the Foundation, who dropped by whenever it suited him. He had mumbled something about digging up bugs or insects, Mrs Yeager was unsure which.

Of course, Sean's father was still missing, presumed lost on Foundation business. Although Sean had not seen him since he was three, he would often ask about his father, which never failed to bring tears to Mrs Yeager's eyes. As for the much-wanted dog, they had resorted to borrowing other people's pets from time to time. It had felt strange at first, but returning them without drama or expense was a definite bonus.

Sean was an inquisitive and restless teenager. He lived a normal life in an unremarkable town and attended a mundane, yet slightly eccentric, senior school. He was tall for his age and good at sport when he chose to be, although he preferred keeping his mind active. He was an only child and, outside of school, he liked to play strategy games on his computer. His favourite was Conquest of the Vuloz, a galactic campaign with real-time battles.

In an unguarded moment, Sean's thoughts returned to school, and he winced. The prospect of sitting through hours of dull lessons was not appealing, though he looked forward to seeing his friends again. He wondered where they had been during the long summer holidays.

'Have you seen my phone anywhere?' said Mrs Yeager, hanging up her raincoat. 'I could have sworn I left it on the table.'

'Perhaps aliens took it?' said Sean, slumping full-length on a faded sofa in the living room.

'Do you really think aliens would come all this way *just* to steal my phone?' said Mrs Yeager, scouring the room.

'Yeah, they're invisible, and they're camping in the back garden, didn't you know?' said Sean, rising to join the search.

'They'd better not phone home,' said Mrs Yeager. 'Not on *my* tariff.'

Sean stood bolt upright in the middle of the living room. He tensed, and the veins in his neck began to throb.

'*Where* is my Dreampad? I was about to liberate another planet.'

'I don't know, Sean. Have you tried looking for it?'

'You've hidden it again, *haven't* you?'

'Perhaps you left it in your room?' said Mrs Yeager.

In truth, she wished aliens *had* broken in and stolen the Dreampad. Not her phone, that was far too important. But if a game kept him busy, where was the harm? No, on second thoughts it would be better if aliens had thrown the Dreampad into a black hole on Conquest of the Nerdwasters or whatever it was called. Perhaps then, Sean would focus on his homework and behave like a normal human being?

'He's like his father,' she thought. 'Always tinkering around with gadgets. Right, *phone*, where are you? I simply *cannot* afford to lose my contacts and messages. Sean, help me look for it will you?'

Her plea hung in the air, unanswered.

Sean charged upstairs like a hungry lion chasing a wildebeest. He flung open his bedroom door and dived under his bed. It was empty.

'Where are my crates?' he cried, his heart racing.

The only signs of his most cherished possessions were some dusty grooves in the carpet. His Dreampad and charger were gone. His books were gone. His prized collection of comics and model cars had vanished. Even Rise of the Ultrabulous One, a rare collector's edition left by his father, was missing. Sean let out a snarl, and his heart began to pound.

'If Mum's taken my stuff...'

'What's all the fuss about?' said Mrs Yeager, joining him.

'What have you done with my crates?' said Sean.

'You know I would never take your...'

Mrs Yeager's lower lip quivered in mid-sentence. She stood, motionless and stared at the wall, captivated. Sean followed her gaze. There, above the bed was a large, circular hole where the bedroom wall should have been. It was like a perfect round window, without glass. Around its edges, bricks and plaster had been cut clean through to reveal yellow fluffs of insulation. Sean froze in disbelief. He watched people walk up and down the pavement, holding half-open umbrellas at the ready. In the distance, a black cat tiptoed across the road and avoided the puddles.

'Where are my posters? And what happened to the wall?'

'I'm calling the police,' said Mrs Yeager. 'They'll know what to do.'

Sean crawled across the bed and craned his neck out of the hole, hoping to find his belongings on the ground. He felt a breeze on his face and a warm flash of sunlight.

'When I find out who did this, I'll…'

'Sean! Get away from there!' said Mrs Yeager.

He felt his ankles being tugged back, and the duvet ruffled beneath him.

'They've taken everything! How am I going to chat with my friends? How am I going to play any games? How am I going to have any fun?'

'It's okay, Sean, we can replace them,' said Mrs Yeager, attempting a clumsy embrace.

Sean wriggled free.

'You don't understand! No one understands! Dad left me those comics. They're all I have left,' said Sean, with tears running down his face.

Apart from a handful of old photographs, Sean felt no connection with his father. He could not remember meeting him, and yet he still felt a sense of loss. He wanted to know what his father was like and to spend time with him. He had tried asking his mother, but she usually started crying. In the end, he gave up and turned to his comics and games. He imagined his father was an action hero who had saved a town but was unable to save himself. It was a tragic version of events, yet somehow it made him feel more at ease.

Daylight turned to dusk, and there was a sharp crack of thunder, followed by rain. The sudden downpour was like a bath tap opening on high. Specks of water blew sideways and settled on Sean's face. In horror, he dragged his mother from the room and slammed the bedroom door.

'And who's going to replace my wall?'

Mrs Yeager wandered off and returned with a telephone handset on loudspeaker.

'Which emergency service do you require?' said a serious voice.

'And where is your father when we need him?' she said, in Sean's general direction.

Sean growled at this slight on his father's character and was about to protest when the operator replied.

'I'm sorry, what did you say?'

'Oh, err, police.'

****

Agent Lee leapt in her chair like someone had poked her with a cattle prod. She roused a yawning colleague and addressed him in her bossiest tone.

'Wake up! There's been a security breach! We have to do something. Now!'

'Yeah, sure. I'm on it.'

Her colleague squinted and stabbed commands into a keyboard.

'Alert! Code ten! Alert! Code ten!' flashed a bank of computer screens in front of them. Speakers repeated the words in unison. Soon, communicators were buzzing and beeping on the wrists and necks of every Foundation agent in the building. Commandos ran around brandishing weapons and looking for locations to guard. This was the first time in years a security alert had been set off. In every room and corridor at the Foundation's Headquarters, people looked at each other, unsure what to do next. Or what 'code ten' actually meant.

'This is Brigadier Cuthbertson, where is this 'code ten', Control?'

'We have a break-in at the home of a priority-one subject, sir.'

'Who is it?'

'Sean Yeager, sir,' said Lee, shaking.

'Who's that?' said Cuthbertson. 'This had better be a tree-rat biting through a cable, or heads will roll. And if I catch

5

another squirrel digging up my lawn...'

Lee broke out in a cold sweat. It was unlike the Brigadier to take an interest in security or any other details for that matter.

'How did they get in?'

'It looks like they cut a hole through an upstairs wall, sir.'

Or to be more precise, they had removed a perfect, brick circle from the upper side-wall of a quiet, residential home in broad daylight. Why on her shift? And what on Earth had they used to cut such a large hole, undetected?

'I want live pictures. And get our nearest team over there on the double. I want the whole area secured, do you hear me?'

'I would, sir, but our spy-bots are not responding. I'm using a satellite to zoom in on the house.'

'Then patch those pictures through to me! I want a full report before lunchtime,' said Cuthbertson.

'I'll order a lock-down right away, sir.'

Lee tried to remember the Yeager family and shook her head. It mattered little, duty called. She sighed, relieved it would be someone else's mess to sort out. Not to mention the endless paperwork. The Foundation didn't tolerate failure, ever. Not since the St Jacobs incident, which no one dared to mention in case they were somehow blamed. According to the rumour mill, it had resulted in a volcanic eruption and the destruction of half an island.

'Where is this *Sean Yeager*?' said Cuthbertson.

'We think he went shopping, sir.'

There was a long pause.

'Oops,' she thought. 'Wrong answer.'

'We think? We *think*? Someone had better know! He's meant to be under twenty-four-hour protection. Collect all our video and tracking data for the last forty-eight hours. I want to know *exactly* how a burglar broke into a protected house, on *your* watch.'

'Yes, sir. Right away, sir.'

Lee felt her cheeks flush. She swivelled in her chair and

summoned another colleague. Now she understood why Cuthbertson was nicknamed Hard Cheese. He had a point though, to be fair. Priority-one subjects were meant to be under constant guard. And how *did* someone dissolve half a house without setting off any alarms? The Foundation had video cameras, tremor detectors and spy-bots patrolling the site.

Her second-in-command perched himself beside her.

'Call Surveillance; we need all their data on the Yeager house for the past two days.'

'Right away, ma'am.'

Lee winced at the prospect of reviewing hours and hours of video footage.

****

About six miles from the Yeager house, two Foundation agents sat in a booth at an old-fashioned diner. Clavity was a thickset man with a big appetite. He had waited for his club sandwich and onion rings for literally minutes. It had been an early start, and his empty stomach demanded food. The moment his order arrived he grabbed it with two shovel-sized hands and took the largest bite he could manage.

His partner, Agent Rusham, sipped mineral water and eyed him with a look of disdain. She smoothed her bob of jet-black hair behind one ear and made a bet with herself that Clavity would not make his sixtieth birthday. Not with all the rubbish he ate. She was fond of Clavity like an eccentric, uncle, but would he listen to her advice about food and exercise? It was as likely as him being promoted to Sigma Force. She, on the other hand, was going all the way to the top, whatever it took.

The agents' wrist and neckpieces came alive, beeping and buzzing in time. Clavity ignored his and took another bite of his triple-decker sandwich.

'Major, we have a code ten alert!' said Rusham, rising from her seat. 'This is no time for gorging yourself. We need to

7

fuse atoms and ship out.'

Clavity shrugged and took another bite. His mouth was crammed, and he took an age to answer.

'It's probably another false alarm. Can't it wait a few more minutes?'

'Shall we?' said Rusham, wearing her coldest frown.

Clavity threw some money on the table and brought the rest of his brunch with him. He caught the restaurant's door with his right boot, an inch before it flattened his nose. He grumbled about his untouched coffee and left the diner.

Rusham had reached the car, and Clavity hurried after her splashing through the puddles. For a stocky man, he moved surprisingly well when he set his mind on it. He landed sideways in the passenger seat and missed head-butting his partner by a whisker. Rusham, however, did not even blink. She was used to her partner's clumsiness, and his shambolic ways amused her.

'Who is this priority-one subject anyway?' said Clavity, between mouthfuls.

'Sean Yeager. And this is *serious*. The intruder might still be on the premises, and Cuthbertson is having a fit.'

'Why?' said Clavity, shrugging.

'Because, Major,' said Rusham, stretching her neck to the vanity mirror. '*We* were meant to be there *all* morning!'

'Oops,' said Clavity.

Rusham lifted her sunglasses and stared into a retina scanner for a few seconds. She had deep, brown eyes with a tawny green outer rim, a gift from her father's side.

'Welcome, Agent Rusham,' said a warm, female voice.

Hermes burst into life. In a whirr of turbines, Rusham reversed out into the street and sped away

Their white sports car attracted plenty of admiring glances as it cruised through a leafy suburb. Most people mistook Clavity and Rusham for property developers or city traders. It was an unusual disguise, but it seemed to work.

'HQ has intercepted an emergency call to the police,' said Rusham. 'They're sending over a patrol car.'

'I'll stand down our friends in blue with a quick phone call,' said Clavity. 'Best if they don't start snooping around.'

'And best if they don't beat us to it,' said Rusham, with a wry smile.

In theory, Clavity was in charge.

'But look who's driving the hi-tech car,' thought Rusham, as she weaved in and out of the traffic.

CHAPTER 2: WATCHING

On a distant world, a bell-like tone rang out in the sleeping quarters of Deijan Klesus.

'Bong! Urgent report for Deijan Klesus. Bong! Urgent report for Deijan Klesus.'

Klesus grumbled to himself. He never seemed to have a moment's peace since the latest campaign began.

'Go ahead, Alviqua,' he said, in a resigned voice.

He dreaded receiving messages. Had another planetary system fallen? Could he spare any more valuable forces to engage the enemy? There was never any good news. He was sure the sentients kept it all to themselves.

A hologram appeared in the centre of his bedroom. It was a high-resolution figure of a woman wearing a blue jumpsuit.

'Sentient SB-12-59 wishes to report.'

'Yes, 12-59, what is it?' said Klesus, reaching for an inhaler.

The war was playing havoc with his stomach.

'Ulcers,' his droid-doctor said. 'Take some rest,' it said.

'You try running a pan-galactic war and taking a holiday,' was his usual reply.

The hologram displayed a simulated face for his benefit and its own amusement. The face smiled.

'Greetings, Deijan, we have important news.'

Klesus shrugged. Wasn't it always important? Why else would the sentients disturb him when he was trying to sleep? They were always awake, always processing, and he was certain they never once considered his health.

'Yes, 12-59, what is your news?'

'We have found what you were looking for, Deijan. On Terra Prime.'

Klesus sucked on a tube of medicine and let anti-stress vapour soothe his lungs. Great, another cryptic message.

They were his favourite, especially when he was trembling with fatigue. He tried to remember any missions he had sent to Terra Prime. Blank. Nada. Nothing. It was a young planet of no strategic importance. For a start, it was light-years from anywhere.

'What have you found, 12-59? And please make it brief.'

He knew a spy-bot was unlikely to hurry a message across several hundred light-years of folded space-time. He would be lucky to have any rest for hours, let alone the deep sleep he craved.

'We have found anomalies,' said 12-59.

'What kind of anomalies? Explain.'

This could go on all night. An anomaly might be a meteorite strike, a change in the weather or a new form of life. It could be almost anything.

'Technical and biological anomalies,' continued the spy-bot.

Klesus felt a jolt in his heart. This was unheard of. Terra Prime was a backward planet in dire need of an idea to call its own. Next, this spy-bot would be claiming the Terrans had invented a miracle weapon. Perhaps they had created a vaccine to wipe-out the Vuloz? Now that *would* be something.

'More likely the Vuloz have landed and enslaved every one of them,' he said to himself.

'We request a mind upload for evaluation,' continued 12-59, ignoring his mutterings.

Klesus hated mind uploads. The sentients loved to beam millions of details straight into his brain. Sure, it was efficient, but afterwards, the insides of his skull felt like they had been pummelled in an ancient and barbaric contact sport. Which would be fine, if he had the chance to pummel the sentients in return. Evaluation? Decision making would be more accurate. 'What course of action shall we take, Deijan?' 'What are your orders, Deijan?' They were the usual questions.

Sentient computers were capable of gathering enough information to fill a gas giant, but could they make a decision? Nope. With them, it was either verify information or launch all-out destruction. Which was why they had been relieved of command many years ago, and not before time. You need a strategy to defeat an enemy as cunning and adaptable as the Vuloz or you lose. And for many centuries now, the Aenaids *had* been losing, despite the sentients. What Klesus needed more than anything was a fresh approach to outwit his mortal enemy.

'Confirm you have reliable information,' he said, staggering to the living area.

'We have verified our data with many sources including carbon and silica-based life forms,' said 12-59.

Which meant 12-59 had been up to the spy-bots' usual trick of mind-probing life forms and breaking into primitive computer systems. It was considered unethical if you asked the legal-bots. However, in times of war, the Deijan considered it a necessary evil. Besides, the Terrans would not even know it had happened.

'And why should I care about these anomalies?'

Klesus realised that even the most advanced spy-bot would struggle to answer this question. 12-59 was probably hundreds of years old already and obsolete by modern standards. There was a long pause. Klesus reached for a chemo-patch to treat his inevitable headache.

'Might as well make this painless,' he thought.

'We believe we have found traces of the missing scout ship,' said 12-59, in a steady tone. 'With a probability of 92%.'

Klesus fell into a reclining chair and clutched his chest. The sentients would not let him die, no matter how hard his body tried to give in. He was now more than three thousand years old and kept alive against his wishes.

'*The* scout ship?' he said. At last, a chance to end this infernal war. A chance to restore the Aenaid race to their rightful place and finally get some sleep.'

Klesus slumped back, while nanobots worked their magic and repaired his heart from the inside. The moment he was revived, images and voices flashed into his mind. It was like watching an old-fashioned movie, with the ability to steer the

camera and ask questions. Only in this film, Klesus felt a
steady throb on the inside of his skull. His cortex upgrade
was long overdue, as was his re-cloning.

'Terra Prime is a water-based planet known to the resident
humanoids as Earth,' said the upload.

'Yes, I *know*. What's new?'

It was about time the sentients credited him with some
intelligence, after all the data chips they had planted in his
brain over the centuries.

'Show me these anomalies,' said Klesus, closing his eyes.

Pictures and voices flooded his mind.

'By Ze'us, can you get to the point?' he said, shuddering at
the thought of witnessing every detail of 12-59's report in
four dimensions.

CHAPTER 3: SCRAMBLE

'Clavity, this is Cuthbertson, are you at the Yeager's house yet?'

Cuthbertson sounded angry, perhaps he already knew about their brunch? Clavity gestured to Rusham who shrugged her shoulders and carried on driving. They reached a long queue of traffic and slowed to a crawl.

'How long 'til we get there?'

'In this traffic, about twenty minutes,' said Rusham, checking Hermes' touchscreen.

'We'll be there soon, sir,' said Clavity.

'I don't call twenty minutes soon, Major. Make it five or I'll have you demoted! Over and out.'

'Gee, thanks,' said Clavity.

'What did you expect?' said Rusham. 'We're already late.'

Clavity looked up at the back of a tall, dirty, goods lorry. It moved in fits and starts and towered above them.

'What if we go cross-country?'

'I thought you'd never ask,' said Rusham. 'Hermes, switch to flight mode and hover at ten feet.'

There was a loud whirr and a roar from the rear of the car. Parts slid and clunked into position and they began to rise.

'Camouflage on, hover-mode on,' said Hermes, in a calm voice.

'Err, hang on a minute...' said Clavity, but before he had the chance to finish his sentence, they had turned sharply and were hovering above a hedge.

Clavity knocked his head against the passenger window and let out a groan.

'You could have warned me!'

'I did, Major. By my calculations, we'll be at the Yeager's house in three minutes, thirty,' said Rusham, who was already strapped in.

'Great,' said Clavity, rubbing his ear. 'Can I have my hearing back?'

They sped away and left behind them a chaotic scene.

'Screech!'

The driver who witnessed Hermes' vanishing act braked hard in disbelief.

'Crump!'

His car was rammed from behind by a white van.

'Doof!'

A large, four-wheel drive piled into the white van.

'Smash! Crash! Crunch!'

A long line of vehicles slammed into the back of each other, shedding pieces of light clusters and coloured plastic onto the road. A chorus of car horns sounded, and the drivers found themselves wedged into their seats by airbags.

Unaware of the carnage behind them, Rusham flew Hermes at high-speed above grassy fields. She enjoyed dodging treetops and accelerated over some rising ground.

'Whoa!' said Clavity, as they stampeded a herd of cows and skimmed the top of a wood. 'Do we *have* to fly so low?'

'It's normal procedure, said Rusham. 'We don't want to be spotted, now do we?"

Clavity sighed. He had studied satellite pictures, and the break-in at the Yeager's was no ordinary burglary. If the thieves could remove the side of a house, what could they do to Hermes?

'Right, let's agree on a plan. First, we need to secure the house; then we can call in the clean-up squad. Our spy-bots aren't responding, so we need to be careful. Any questions?'

'Are we going in undercover?' said Rusham.

'Yes, we'll use the stealth gear. The thieves could still be inside the house. I'll smooth things over with Hard Cheese afterwards.'

Rusham raised her eyebrows and whistled.

'Good luck with that one.'

The countryside gave way to scattered buildings as Hermes reached the outskirts of a town.

'We're nearly there,' said Rusham, checking an onscreen map. 'Where do you want to land?'

'First, scan the house on infrared. We can land further up the road,' said Clavity.

While they hovered, the main control screen showed a grey image with two white shapes. Rusham flew past a row of red brick houses and circled back to the road. Clavity studied the images.

'There are two life signs inside the house but no one else on the premises.'

'Prepare for landing,' said Rusham.

A short distance from the Yeager's house, Hermes threw down a torrent of hot air and descended vertically into an empty parking space. It almost flattened a black cat that was rolling its back on the road. Fortunately for the cat, the down-draught was so fierce it blew the feline sideways into a garden. The cat righted itself and staggered away in a daze.

'Major, your orders are to secure the area and no heroics, do you hear me?' said Cuthbertson.

'Yes, sir,' said Clavity.

Clavity and Rusham opened a locker inside Hermes and selected an array of gear. They twisted and contorted to pull on their stealth suits in the confirmed space.

'Set blasters to stun,' said Clavity. 'Ready?'

Rusham gave a thumbs-up.

Rusham and Clavity climbed out of Hermes and appeared as if out of nowhere, in a quiet, residential road. A young mother approached pushing a baby buggy. She shook her head and broke into a trot. Meanwhile, Hermes closed its doors and vanished.

Clavity and Rusham took opposite sides of the road and strode towards the Yeager house. Hidden from the naked eye, they reflected a blurred image of the scenery around them. Clavity watched Rusham through a special visor. She knelt and pulled a device from her body armour. She swept it through the air several times and studied a read-out.

'Anything on the scanner?' said Clavity.

17

'Nothing much, but I'm picking up a strange background reading.'

'Alright, I'm going in. Cover me.'

'Yes, sir!'

Clavity ran towards the Yeager's house. He bounded across their front lawn and took off. With his hover-pack on full blast, he climbed up the front of the house and soared above its roof.

'What in blazes are you doing, Clavity?' said Cuthbertson.

'Securing the area, sir.'

Clavity hovered over a chimney and swept the garden with his scanner.

'Clear on UV, infrared and radar. If anyone's hiding down there they have better gear than us.'

Next, he turned his attention to the side of the house. It was an ordinary dwelling with a large, oval hole where its bedroom wall should have been.

'I'm surprised the roof hasn't caved in,' said Clavity.

He hovered down the side of the house and peered into an exposed bedroom. A boy wearing a bright blue t-shirt stood behind a bed and waved at him. Clavity's communicator fell silent. He flew around the house and landed beside the front door.

'How did that boy see me? I'm invisible!'

Rusham arrived, grinning, and gave him a nudge on the arm.

'Having fun playing the hero?' she said, turning away from Clavity and scanning the street.

'What's your status, Major?' said Cuthbertson, in a haughty tone.

'All clear?' said Clavity.

'Yes, sir. And totally invisible,' said Rusham.

'We're ready for the clean-up squad,' said Clavity.

'Shame about your power pack,' whispered Rusham. 'I bet the neighbours will be phoning the police by now.'

Clavity gulped.

Further down the road, two men sat in an immaculate red van. They watched Clavity on a pop-up screen and steered a camera drone with a tiny joystick.

'You see that, Greerbo? You see what we're up against?' snarled a thin, bearded man, with penetrating eyes. 'I told you we were too slow, but would you listen?'

'Yes, boss. I mean, no, boss. Shall we leave now, boss?'

Greerbo was a short, stocky man, with an ugly face. His twisted nose was the result of one too many brawls.

'Not yet, we don't want to attract attention, now do we?' said Krankhausen.

The men continued to watch Clavity. After a few minutes, Greerbo could hold his tongue no longer.

'I still don't get it, boss. If the kid's so important, why don't we kidnap him? It would be much easier.'

Krankhausen looked as though he might explode with rage. Instead, an evil smile stretched across his face.

'Greerbo, are you questioning my judgement?'

'Err, no, boss. I was just wondering.'

'You see these piles of junk?' said Krankhausen, gesturing at several crates on the floor behind them.

'Yes, boss?'

'They don't need feeding, they won't scream and most importantly they won't try and escape,' said Krankhausen.

He reached into a crate and pulled out a brush matted with brown hair.

'*This* is our prize, Greerbo. All we need are a few strands of that Yeager brat's DNA and Deveraux will pay me a fortune.'

CHAPTER 4: INVESTIGATION

The Yeager's front door swung open.

'That's him!' said Sean, pointing at Clavity.

'What are you playing at, clambering all over my roof?' said Mrs Yeager.

'Err, police, ma'am,' said Clavity, taking off his helmet. 'We're investigating a break-in.'

'Police, eh?' said Mrs Yeager. 'Can I see your badge?'

Clavity fumbled in his pocket and produced a black wallet containing a gold shield. Beneath the shield, a green light flashed in a rhythmic pattern.

'Do you think I'm an idiot?' said Mrs Yeager.

Clavity frowned. The hypnotic circuits in Foundation identity badges were strong enough to put a gorilla into a trance. They were potent enough to convince most people Clavity was a tap-dancing mouse if necessary.

'I mean, do the police carry MPA280 blasters?' she said, pointing at the weapon on Clavity's hip. 'And by the way, those hypnotic badges have never worked on me.'

Clavity winced and heard Rusham chuckle beside him, still hidden by her camouflage.

'And do the police wear anti-gravity hover packs with light field reflector plates and I'm guessing…a flat battery pack?'

'I, uh…'

Clavity cleared his throat to explain, but words failed him. This time he was well and truly busted. He watched Sean study him from head to toe and felt like an exhibit in a museum. It was unnerving.

'Is your camera on?' said Mrs Yeager, waving her hand in front of Clavity's visor. 'Brigadier, can you call off the goon squad and send over some builders to repair my house?'

Clavity's phone rang; he answered, before handing it to Mrs Yeager.

'The Brigadier would like a word, ma'am.'

'Ah, Brigadier, how good to hear from you. If I remember correctly, you promised I would never see your little helpers ever again?'

'I'm sorry, Mrs Yeager, we still need to keep an eye on you.'

'And a great job you're doing too. Where exactly *is* the rest of my house?'

'Hmm, I can understand if you're a little upset...'

'And what about my husband? Have you managed to find him yet?'

'Err, not as such. Look, Mrs Yeager, if we can we just take a look around, I'm sure we can come to some arrangement?'

Mrs Yeager sighed. What choice did she have? If she allowed the Foundation back into her life, she would probably find them nosing around in her garden in the middle of the night. On the other hand, what about the bedroom wall?

'Alright, I'll agree on one condition – that you repair my house, today.'

Mrs Yeager shook her head in disbelief. For all she knew it was the Foundation who had melted her wall in the first place. But why would they? Then again, why was one of their goons climbing all over her roof?

'Agreed,' said Cuthbertson. 'Can you pass me back to Major Clavity?'

Mrs Yeager handed Clavity the phone and gave him a withering look. He nodded sheepishly in apology.

'Yes, Brigadier, loud and clear. We'll secure the area right away.'

As he spoke, a small, blue car drove past and pulled into an empty parking space further along the road.

'Crunch!'

Its bonnet crumpled like tin foil and caved in on itself. The car rolled backwards for a moment and radiator fluid gushed onto the road. The car came to a halt, and its front grill clattered to the ground. Clavity let out a groan and almost dropped his phone. Hermes flickered into sight and wailed a siren in disapproval at the offending vehicle. Its bodywork was gleaming and unmarked.

'Can you go and sort things out, Rusham?' said Clavity.

Rusham appeared beside him, to the obvious surprise of the Yeagers.

'Yes, I'd love to,' she replied, sarcastically. 'Is there anything else you'd like me to clear up, your highness?'

Clavity gave her a 'just do it' stare, and Rusham shook her head. She strutted across the road in a huff. Halfway across, she stopped and hurried back to the house, waving her scanner.

'What is it now?' said Clavity.

'Ionic radiation,' said Rusham. 'And it's coming from nearby.'

As she spoke, a red van crawled past, and the scanner beeped louder.

'Fetch Hermes,' said Clavity.

Rusham gave him a dirty look.

'But what about Cuthbertson?'

'I'll explain everything later.'

'On your head be it,' said Rusham, sprinting across the road.

Sean wandered after her, keen to see the agent's car. Halfway across the road, he was distracted by a howling noise from the red van. It performed a clumsy U-turn, before accelerating towards him like a dragster, its wheels spinning and smoking wildly.

'Watch out!' cried Clavity.

Sean leapt to one side, and the van sped past, missing him by a hair's breadth. He watched in disbelief as the van raced away.

'You maniac!' he cried.

Clavity pulled out a sidearm and took aim.

'Better not,' he thought. Today had been bad enough already without risking the neighbourhood. His knowledge on the subject was shaky, but Clavity was pretty sure a blaster beam and ionic radiation would cause an explosion.

The van skidded around the stricken, blue car and howled away down the road.

'Great reactions,' said Clavity, offering Sean a hand.

Before Sean could reply, Hermes arrived and almost ran over Clavity.

'Hey!' he cried, leaping out of the way.

The passenger door rose like a wing.

'Hop in!' said Rusham.

'Fancy a trip?' said Clavity.

Sean considered his options. Should he stay at home and let the thieves get away? Or should he trust the strangers and their high-tech car? It was a tough decision.

'Did they steal my Dreampad? And my comics?' said Sean.

Clavity gave a shrug.

'There's only one way to find out.'

'And they're getting away!' said Rusham.

'Let's get them!' said Sean, climbing into the passenger seat.

Clavity groaned and clambered into the back.

'Take it easy, Rusham. By the book, eh?'

This was possibly the worst day of his career, including the St Jacobs incident. He dreaded to think what Cuthbertson would say when he returned to headquarters. It was unlikely to be pleasant.

'Sean Yeager! Come back here this instant!' cried Mrs Yeager.

Sean could just about make out his mother's voice, but her words were lost in the roar of Hermes' engine as it screeched away.

'Someone broke my car,' said an elderly gentleman, staggering towards her. A small trickle of blood dribbled down his cheek, and his face was ghostly white.

'Did you see?'

Mrs Yeager sighed.

'Come in, and have a cup of tea, Mr Shawcross. And let's have a look at your cut.'

She prayed Sean would be safe and vowed to give Cuthbertson a stern talking to when she found her phone.

****

'Clavity, what's going on?'

It was Cuthbertson, and by now he was probably having his third kitten. Clavity adjusted his neckpiece.

'We're heading east in pursuit of a suspect. Rusham detected an ionic drive.'

'Major, I told you to protect the Yeagers!'

'Sean Yeager is with us now, sir.'

There was an audible gasp.

'You've taken him *with* you? And what about Mrs Yeager?'

'I believe she's talking to the clean-up squad, sir.'

'Who's that?' said Sean.

'Our boss,' whispered Rusham, putting a finger to her lips.

She turned onto a busy road in pursuit of the red van. It sped away and began to rise above the traffic. Its sides folded outwards into triangular wings, and its rear doors parted to reveal three cone-shaped exhausts. In a burst of flames, the van rose into the sky and was gone. In its wake, a sports car crashed into a parked vehicle and smoke poured from its paintwork.

'Watch out!' said Clavity.

'I'm on it,' said Rusham, steering around the burning car and turning off the main road.

Cuthbertson returned on the intercom.

'Major, do I have to tell you how many regulations…blah,

blah, blah, blah, blah…'

But Clavity was preoccupied watching Hermes' scanner.

'We are tracking a flying van, accelerating away from our position and heading due south. Permission to engage, sir?'

'Flying van?' said Cuthbertson. 'Control, do you have anything on your radar?'

There was a pause and some muffled conversations at HQ.

'Vanished? Where?' said Cuthbertson. 'Okay, Clavity, follow them but do not engage. Repeat, do not engage. Do you hear me?'

'Will do, sir,' said Clavity, leaning between the front seats. 'You heard the man, Rusham. Do you have their heading?'

'We should be able to track them using our sensors,' said Rusham.

She steered Hermes into a quiet, residential road lined with cherry trees.

'Belts on everyone.'

Sean pulled a Y-shaped harness over his shoulders and clicked it into a circular clasp.

'Cool, wait 'til my friends hear about this.'

'Best keep it to yourself, Sean,' said Clavity. 'We'll talk about it later. Okay, Rusham, you know what to do.'

Rusham busied herself at the controls.

'Hermes, engage camouflage. Switch to flight mode and hover at thirty feet.'

'Flight mode confirmed,' said a calm, female voice.

Motors whirred and wing pieces slid into position as Hermes rose above the trees. Sean watched stabiliser fins extend from the front of the car and heard the wheel arches seal up.

'What does this button do?' he said, eyeing a bright red control on the dashboard.

'Don't touch anything!' said Rusham.

But Sean could not help himself. Intrigued by its texture, he ran a finger over the shiny, red button. At once, there was a loud roar, and he was thrown back in his seat.

'Ahhh!'

Sean's cheeks quivered like jellies, and his neck strained with acceleration. Behind him, Clavity was thrown across the rear seat, his seatbelt flapping.

'Sorry,' said Sean.

Rusham regained control and wiped her brow. She gave an unconvincing smile.

'Right, we're still alive. Master Yeager, I need you to keep your hands in your pockets. Do *not* touch anything. Do you understand?'

Embarrassed and shaken, Sean gave a silent nod.

'I'm alright. Don't worry about me,' said a voice behind them.

Rusham raised her eyes to the ceiling.

'Hermes, switch to ionic scan and track the course of a bandit heading south.'

'Confirmed,' said Hermes.

A colourful map appeared on the inside of the windscreen. It showed a green trail stretching out before them against rolling contours of land and coastline. The bandit was now a distant, orange dot near the edge of the display.

'Ouch, my neck,' said Clavity.

'Having a good flight, Major?' said Rusham.

'Wonderful, thanks. Any sign of that van?'

'We're on its trail.'

'And it's escaping!' said Sean.

'Not for long,' said Rusham.

Cuthbertson's voice returned on the intercom.

'Clavity, what in blazes are you doing? I've had the Fire Brigade on the phone complaining about some trees you roasted!'

Sean felt himself blush and gazed at the landscape below. He felt Rusham glowering in his direction.

CHAPTER 5: PURSUIT

Hermes' instrument panel flickered.

'Can you see where the bandit's gone?' said Clavity.

'They're fifty nautical miles away and increasing,' said Rusham. 'If we don't do something, we're going to lose them.'

'How much fuel do we have left?'

'Enough,' said Rusham. 'Do you want to risk it?'

Clavity considered the situation for a moment. If the van escaped, so did their best chance of catching the burglar. Or was it a coincidence that a sky-van powered by an ionic drive had left the Yeager's house in a hurry?

'Fuse some atoms!' said Clavity. 'We can't let those joyriders get away with it.'

'Brace yourselves. Engaging particle-drive in three, two, one.'

Hermes shuddered as they picked up speed, and Sean felt his stomach squeeze.

'This is better than a roller coaster!' he cried.

'It sure is,' said Rusham, grinning.

In a few minutes, the van became a steady blip in the centre of the windscreen. Sean noticed a distant speck ahead of them cruising below the clouds.

'We have visual contact, Major,' said Rusham.

'Have you gone completely mad?' said Cuthbertson, on the intercom. 'Half the country's heard a sonic boom, and I've had the Air Force on the phone telling me they've launched fighters to intercept you!'

'We're pursuing the van, sir,' said Rusham.

'Did it occur to you to engage stealth mode, Agent Rusham? Or have you broken that as well?'

'Yes, sir.'

'It occurred to you or you've broken it?' said Cuthbertson.

'Both, sir,' said Rusham. 'Major?'

Clavity leaned forwards and whispered.

'Tell him we're in hot pursuit of the burglar.'

'You're lighting up our tracking screen like a rash on a baby's bottom,' said Cuthbertson.

'Missile alert. Missile alert. Range three thousand metres and closing,' said Hermes, in her usual calm manner.

'Take evasive action!' said Clavity, hurrying to strap himself in.

Rusham threw Hermes sideways and upwards into a vertical climb.

'Missile lock. Missile lock,' said Hermes.

'Hermes, deploy counter-measures,' said Rusham.

There was a burst on either side of the vehicle, and Hermes threw out debris. Having gained height, Rusham steered Hermes into a right turn followed by a steep dive. Sean watched a patchwork of green become fields and hedges at an alarming pace. His body weight hung forwards, held in place by the seatbelt.

'I think I'm going to be sick.'

'Save it for later,' said Rusham.

Hermes instrument panel lit up.

'Ground warning. Ground warning.'

At the last second, Rusham pulled out of their dive and banked hard to the left.

'Boom!' 'Boom!'

Two missiles exploded above the ground, and Hermes rocked.

'Phew, that was close,' said Rusham, levelling out and setting a new course.

'Great job,' said Clavity. 'Can we still track the van?'

'Their missile trails should lead us back to them,' said Rusham, accelerating Hermes once more.

A new voice crackled on the intercom.

'Enjoying your ride, you bumbling idiots? Follow me if you dare!'

The speaker clicked and fell silent.

'Who in tarnation is that?' said Clavity.

'Our missile-wielding friend I expect,' said Rusham. 'Whoever it is they've blocked our communications. We're on our own, Major.'

'I think he's called Krank-hausen,' said Sean. In his mind, he pictured a bearded face and penetrating eyes. He felt a queasy shudder ripple through his body.

'Von Krankhausen?' said Clavity. 'I thought we caught that old goat years ago?'

'We did. But he escaped, and no one's seen him for years,' said Rusham. 'How come you know about him, Sean?'

'It just came to me,' said Sean, staring out of the window.

'Hermes, run a voice match on the bandit's message,' said Rusham.

'Affirmative.'

Sean watched the blip move closer. Beneath them, land gave way to grey water and tiny flecks of white.

'The bandit's voice matches Egbert Von Krankhausen, visual on screen now,' said Hermes.

Sean trembled as a cruel face appeared on the central screen. It was a middle-aged man with dark hair and a pointed goatee. He held a black and white numbered board in front of his chest.

'Do you recognise him, Sean?' said Rusham.

The face had the same dark eyes and pallid skin, but the man's hair seemed longer and darker than he imagined.

'Sort of, but his hair looks different.'

'Radar lock. Radar lock,' said Hermes, in its familiar, laid-back voice.

'Here we go again,' said Clavity.

'Not so fast, Krankhausen,' said Rusham. 'Hermes, engage lasers, full power.'

'Confirmed,' said the calm voice.

'You heard Cuthbertson; we can't shoot him down,' said Clavity.

'Yeah? Well, I'm not going to be shot down either,' said

31

Rusham.

Clavity tried to stretch between the seats but was unable to reach any controls. The tracking display flashed and went blank.

'Now where's he gone?'

'Hermes, show the bandit's last position,' said Rusham.

'On screen now.'

'They can't be,' said Clavity. 'That's underground!'

'Not underground, Major. Underwater.'

Rusham put Hermes into a shallow dive and reduced their speed, while Clavity pulled on his harness. Hermes slowed until it was hovering just above the water.

'Switch to underwater mode,' said Rusham. 'Hold tight everyone, here we go!'

Hermes skimmed the waves, and hydraulic motors adjusted its control surfaces. A few seconds later, they tipped head-first into the sea with a giant splash. When the bubbles had cleared, a pair of fan motors hummed behind them. Outside there was nothing but a dark, blue fog of seawater.

'No sign of the bandit on sonar,' said Rusham.

'Do we have a thermal trace?' said Clavity.

'No, the seawater's too dense. Any ideas?'

'Enjoying your swim?' said a familiar voice. 'Adieu, Foundation fools!'

Sean and Rusham glanced at each other.

'I have a bad feeling about this,' said Sean.

'What do you mean?' said Rusham.

Before Sean could reply, a sonar pip echoed around them. It bounced against Hermes and reflected away into the ocean. It was followed by a deep thud. The lights went out, and they found themselves sitting in darkness, with only the creaks and groans of Hermes' hull for company.

'Our controls are dead!' said Rusham.

A faint, red lamp came on, yielding barely enough light to see. The screens were blank, and the fan motors were silent.

'Hermes?' said Rusham, 'Hermes?'

Her question hung in the air, unanswered.

They began to drift and sank further into the gloomy depths.

'We can't just sit here,' said Sean.

Rusham woke from her daze.

'Prepare for emergency flotation. In three, two, one.'

Rusham flipped a cover back beneath the steering column and flicked a switch. After a short delay, bubbles rushed from pods on either side, and Hermes jerked upwards.

'I hope this works,' said Clavity.

Hermes broke through the surface in a mass of foam and bounced around for a while. Large, white floats encircled the vehicle, and it began to rise and fall on the waves. Sean let out a sigh as warm, yellow sunlight filled the car. For a few minutes, no one spoke.

'Ye gads, what's that?' said Clavity.

To their left, a large, white and blue shape loomed above the sea. Several stories tall, it was heading towards them on a collision course.

'It's a ship. Dive! Dive!' said Clavity.

'We can't, Major. We have no power.'

The ship continued on its course and sounded a deep horn.

'It's a ferry,' said Sean.

'And ferries don't change course for anyone,' said Clavity. 'How do we open the roof?'

'We can't, Major, it's pressurised. All we can do is blast our way out, which would probably sink us. Besides, what are we going to do, swim?'

Clavity felt for catches on the ceiling.

'There must be a way out?'

'Can't we just open the windows?' said Sean.

Sunlight was replaced by shadows. Soon, they were enclosed on two sides by the enormous twin hulls of a ferry. It was a catamaran, and they listened to an approaching rumble of powerful engines. Hermes bumped against one of the ferry's hulls and burst an airbag. There was a loud scraping noise.

'We've hit something!' said Clavity, to no one in particular. The roar of the ferry's engines drowned out all attempts of conversation. Hermes was dragged backwards by a powerful undercurrent. It clipped something near the ferry's stern and was pulled under, buffeted by the force of a giant propeller. After two of the longest minutes Sean had ever known, Hermes floated back to the surface and was swept away in the ferry's wake.

No one dared to speak until the engine noise had faded. Hermes sagged towards the rear, making its three passengers slump in their seats. They were exhausted but glad to be alive. Sean gazed out at the sky and the sea and felt Hermes bob up and down on the waves. He spotted a dark, triangular shape cutting through the water towards them. He watched it turn and vanish beneath the surface.

'Uh oh, there's a shark out there.'

'Where?' said Rusham, leaning across to take a look.

'I think it went underneath us.'

There was a sharp bump on the underside of the stricken vehicle.

'Woah!' said Clavity.

Sean held his breath and waited for another impact. Instead, a phone buzzed and vibrated on the back seat, making his heart skip a beat.

'Clavity here. Yes, sir. Our mission status?'

Rusham gave a deep sigh.

'We're adrift at sea, being prodded by sharks. No, Krankhausen's got away.'

There were muffled sounds of an angry voice.

'Yes, sir, I realise it's not a fishing trip. Of course, sir.'

Clavity gave a wistful look.

'Yes, sir, I believe our beacon is working. Oh, we're not going anywhere.'

'Unless the sharks eat us,' said Sean.

His words broke the tension, and Rusham let out a chuckle. Clavity joined in, and soon the three of them were laughing. Clavity dropped his phone on the seat, and it switched to speaker mode.

'What did you say? And why are you laughing? I fail to see what's amusing about your predicament. Blah, blah, blah-blah, blah.'

But no one was listening. Clavity ended the call.

'HQ? Who needs 'em, eh?'

'Err, we do, Major,' said Rusham. 'My feet are getting wet.'

CHAPTER 6: DISCOVERY

Agent Lee climbed out of a battered transit van. To the casual passer-by, it was a wreck, but inside it was packed with hi-tech equipment. Lee was unused to field operations and missed her comfortable chair and coffee machine. Still, it was not all bad, at least she could breathe some fresh air and maybe shed a few pounds. Cuthbertson was adamant, he wanted answers about the break-in, and he wanted them right away. Unfortunately, the video footage they had recovered from the Yeager's house was blank. It had either been switched off or someone had blocked the spy-bots' transmissions.

'Right, team, let's get to it. You know the drill. Cuthbertson wants a report in the next two hours,' said Lee.

Her team understood their tasks and hurried into action. The Foundation was under attack for the first time in a decade. They needed clues and needed them fast.

'Hey, get off my flowerbed!' said Mrs Yeager, to a man in blue overalls. She stood on her front doorstep in her flip-flops and had a look of disgust drawn across her face.

'We're from the Gas Board. Someone's reported a leak.'

'Really? Then perhaps you can explain how the gas pipe moved from over there?' said Mrs Yeager, pointing at an exposed, grey pipe jutting out from the garage wall.

'I, err.'

Lee overheard the conversation and came to the aid of her colleague.

'Mrs Yeager, my name is Alison Lee, we're investigating the burglary. Perhaps Brigadier Cuthbertson briefed you?'

Mrs Yeager studied Lee and her badge before smiling.

'Now, Alison, do you have a phone?' she asked, politely.

'Err, yes.'

'Can you do me a *big* favour and call Brigadier

37

Cuthbertson? I'd like a quick chat.'

'Uh, yes of course,' said Lee.

Lee speed-dialled and handed the phone to Mrs Yeager. It rang for a few moments.

'Agent Lee? About time! What have you discovered?'

'Gas pipes and a very angry mother!' said Mrs Yeager.

'Err, what?' said Cuthbertson.

'Where's my son, you old blunderbuss?'

Lee turned pale and tried to recover her phone, but Mrs Yeager shielded it from her.

'Err, who *is* this?'

'The least you could have done is call me!'

'Mrs Yeager? Your uh, son is quite safe. We'll have him home in no time.'

Lee was now worried and called over her team. Quick as a flash, three blue-suited figures surrounded Mrs Yeager. Two held her arms and the other tranquillised her behind her left ear.

'I've been worried sick! Your minions drove off without so much as a...'

In mid-sentence, Mrs Yeager slumped into the agents' arms.

'Take her inside and keep a close eye on her,' said Lee, retrieving her phone.

'Brigadier? Yes, we have everything under control. Can Professor Quark come on site? We have some unusual readings and need his help.'

Behind her, the roof creaked, and a handful of tiles crashed onto the ground. A deep crack appeared above the now infamous hole.

'Oh and Brigadier, we're going to need a team of engineers to prop up the Yeager's house.'

****

'Captain Reynard, come in and take a seat. I have a little

job for you,' said Cuthbertson, sat behind his desk in his private office.

'Yes, sir, how can I help?'

Reynard looked fit and muscular. He wore short-cropped dark hair and a blue and grey camouflaged uniform, complete with a sidearm. He folded his cap carefully between two large hands and sat in a leather armchair.

'First, I need a recovery team to rescue our *elite* agents,' said Cuthbertson. 'They are currently adrift here, in the middle of the ocean. I need them and whatever is left of their vehicle, returned to HQ in one piece.'

'No problem, sir, I have a recovery team on the way,' said Reynard. 'I'm confident we'll find them within the hour.'

'Good,' said Cuthbertson. 'We also need to stop Von Krankhausen once and for all. He's got his hands on some hi-tech equipment, and he's a threat to our operation.'

Reynard nodded gravely.

'I heard he was an ageing has-been, sir?'

'Captain, Von Krankhausen is a mercenary industrialist, and he's dangerous. He escaped from prison last year, and I need him recaptured as soon as possible. The Founder is keen to bring this matter to a rapid conclusion.'

'Understood, sir,' said Reynard. 'Sigma Force is standing by. All we need is his location.'

'Excellent. Oh and one more thing, Captain,' said Cuthbertson, rubbing his moustache. 'Keep a close eye on Clavity and Rusham, will you? Don't let them break anything.'

'I'll attend to it, sir,' said Reynard, smiling.

After Reynard had left, Cuthbertson stalked the hallway in measured strides. He felt a deep sense of unease but was unable to figure out why. He reached an elevator and punched in his passcode. He stared into an eye scanner and activated the elevator's controls.

'Welcome Brigadier, which floor would you like?'

'Laboratory,' he said.

The elevator plunged deep underground and shuddered to

a halt. Two sets of doors opened, and Cuthbertson marched into a bright room filled with equipment.

'Professor, may I have a word?'

A dark-haired man, wearing glasses and a bald patch, sat at a screen studying a graph. He seemed unaware that anyone else was in the room. Around him, technicians buzzed like worker bees, too busy to greet the new arrival.

'Professor? Professor!' said Cuthbertson.

'No need to shout, Henry,' said Quark, adjusting his glasses. 'The readings confirm what we first thought.'

'What readings? What did we think?'

Sometimes Cuthbertson wondered if Quark lived on the same planet as everyone else. Or perhaps he was only visiting?

'There are anti-matter collision artefacts here in the upper spectrum,' said Quark. 'Which, combined with the residual neutrino traces...'

'Professor, I have no idea what you're talking about. What does your gobbledygook mean in plain English?'

Quark paused for a moment and looked almost offended. He lifted his glasses onto his forehead.

'In simple terms, Brigadier, Krankhausen used a Matteract to melt the Yeager's wall.'

'But...' said Cuthbertson, before he was interrupted.

'Yes, he most likely stole it from the Foundation. Which means we also have a security breach,' said Quark. 'By the way, am I still needed at the Yeager house?'

Cuthbertson was speechless and steadied himself on a chair.

'A mole? Here?'

Quark nodded.

'But Krankhausen could kill millions?'

'Well, yes, he is considered to be criminally insane.'

Cuthbertson felt aghast at the news. A whole city might be wiped out in seconds. On *his* watch and using *his* weapons!

'Fortunately, creating anti-matter fuel is likely to be beyond Krankhausen's capabilities,' said Quark.

Cuthbertson raised his eyebrows.

'Why's that?'

'Because he would need a particle accelerator,' said Quark. 'And we know how long it takes to fund one of those, don't we?'

'Thank you, Professor. I need your team to be vigilant. We must find Krankhausen and this mole, as soon as possible.'

'Yes, Brigadier, I have a few ideas,' said Quark, returning to his work. 'Now then,' he said, tapping at his computer.

Cuthbertson felt his legs grow weak and stumbled to the elevator. He returned to his office and used a bug-detector to check every crevice and electrical device. He unplugged all his equipment, including the light fittings and pulled the blinds shut. Safe in the knowledge no one could hear him, he rang Internal Security on an encrypted phone. There was no reply, so he left a voicemail.

'Where in tarnation are you, Jenkins?'

****

Anxious for news about his treasure, Egbert Von Krankhausen led Greerbo to a laboratory at the heart of his base. Below him, the sea washed tirelessly against enormous, steel legs that supported the entire structure and ultimately his plans.

'Have you finished yet?' he demanded of a figure dressed in a white lab coat. 'Make it quick. I'm a busy man.'

Greerbo stood glowering beside him and stretched his arms.

'I have extracted DNA from the hair samples you brought me,' said the technician. 'However, I've encountered a few problems.'

'Problems? I pay you to solve problems not create them.'

Greerbo clicked his knuckles in agreement.

'You see, the base pairs are not, err, normal,' said the technician.

'You'd better make sense quickly, or I'll ask Greerbo here

to teach you how to dive,' said Krankhausen.

The technician's hands began shaking and beads of sweat appeared on his forehead.

'What I mean, sir, is that this DNA has mutated. Instead of *four* base chemicals, or nucleotides, it has at least *six*.'

Krankhausen scowled at the technician and gestured towards Greerbo, who flexed his arms and prepared for action.

'It seems you have a new diving student, Greerbo.'

'Err, what I meant to say, is that this is not normal, human DNA,' said the technician.

'Excellent,' said Krankhausen, smiling. 'Regrettably, your services will not be required today, after all, Greerbo.'

Greerbo sighed and stomped off in the direction of the gym.

'I trust you have some clean samples for me?' said Krankhausen.

The technician swallowed hard.

'I'll make a start on it right away.'

'See that you do,' said Krankhausen, staring out to sea. 'I hear it would take several weeks to swim home.'

****

Agent Lee retrieved a motionless spy-bot from a flowerbed. It was the size of her hand and was covered in rubbery plastic. Crumbs of soil still clung to its outer-skin. It resembled an oversized, mechanical insect with legs, a body and antennae. Lee checked it for signs of damage and found there were none. In normal conditions, spy-bots could run for years on one power pack, but for some reason, this one had seized up. She detached its outer casing and tested its energy cell. It appeared to be fully charged.

'Agent Brown, here's another one. I need you to run a full diagnostic. Let me know as soon as you have the results.'

'Yes, sir,' said Brown, taking it in both hands.

It was the fifth broken spy-bot her team had recovered.

They ranged from burrowers to tree climbers and camouflaged roamers. Each was in good condition, yet none of them showed any signs of life. Brown carried the spy-bot under a tunnel of blue tarpaulin to the field van.

Officially, the Yeager's house was being investigated following a gas explosion. However, passing neighbours decided it was the scene of a crime. And they were not far wrong.

Lee returned to the house and found Mrs Yeager still asleep on the sofa. A medic kept watch and took her pulse every half hour as a precaution. He found it highly irregular and expressed concern about his patient.

Engineers arrived and installed scaffolding and hydraulic jacks to prevent the Yeager's roof from collapsing. They also covered the hole in Sean's bedroom wall with plastic sheeting. It was ugly but effective. The Yeager's house now resembled a building site.

'Professor, I need your help,' said Lee, on the phone. 'Yes, I realise you're busy. Can we at least send you our spy-bot data? No? Why's that? Communications lockdown? On whose orders? Cuthbertson's? Alright, I guess we'll bring our data back on the fun bus. Yes, the van. Okay, see you later. Bye.'

Lee shook her head in frustration.

'A fat lot of help you are,' she muttered, on her way to the van.

'Why would Cuthbertson order a lock-down?' said Brown. 'Are we under attack?'

Lee shrugged.

'Beats me,' she said, keeping her suspicions to herself.

****

Egbert Von Krankhausen was in the middle of an important phone call when Greerbo knocked at his office door.

'Can't you see I'm busy?' he said, muting the line.

'It's our buyer, sir,' said Greerbo. 'He says it's urgent.'

Krankhausen's eyes lit up.

'Thank you, Greerbo. Tell him I'll be along in a moment.'

Krankhausen returned to his phone call and put on his most serious voice.

'As I was saying, either you send me the passcodes I've requested or you won't see your sister for a very long time. Do I make myself clear? Excellent.'

Krankhausen chuckled to himself as he covered the short distance from his office to the conference room.

'Greerbo, our associate needs more convincing. See what ideas you can come up with.'

'Yes, sir,' said Greerbo, leaving the room.

A gaunt face wearing dark glasses filled a large screen on the wall.

'About time, Krankhausen!'

'My apologies, I had an urgent matter to attend to.'

Krankhausen sat at a desk and took out a notebook. The figure on the screen grimaced.

'Look, Krankhausen, I have no intention of paying you ten million dollars in gold for some meagre DNA samples. Why should I when I've already invested billions in your operation?'

Krankhausen was taken aback for a moment. Perhaps he had misjudged the situation?

'It may interest you to know that this DNA came from a Foundation source?'

'Yes, I know and what of it?' said the figure. 'We can kidnap a Foundation agent anytime we like.'

'But you see, this is not *from* a Foundation agent,' said Krankhausen.

'Agent, commando, cook, what difference does it make?'

The figure removed his sunglasses to reveal glaring, red eyes.

'You are trying my patience, Egbert!'

'You don't understand,' said Krankhausen. 'This sample is not human.'

'So where did it come from? A goldfish? A porcupine?'

'No, Mr Deveraux, it's from a Foundation priority-one subject.'

Deveraux stopped smiling. He put his glasses back on and appeared to be typing.

'Bring your samples to the coordinates I'm sending you. Be there tomorrow at twelve hundred hours sharp. And don't be late, Egbert, or the next time we'll meet will be at your funeral.'

The screen went blank, leaving Krankhausen alone and his heartbeat racing.

'Yes, Mr Deveraux. Whatever you say.'

CHAPTER 7: CLUES

Sean and Agent Rusham took a seat in a waiting room at the Foundation Medical Centre. A doctor returned carrying a tablet computer.

'It's good news, you're in great health.'

'Phew,' said Sean.

'But I must say you have an unusual genetic profile,' said the doctor.

'What do you mean?'

'Oh, it's nothing to worry about,' said a tall man, who appeared beside them, as if from nowhere.

'Founder?' said Rusham, rising to salute.

'Please, call me Cassius.'

The Founder, Cassius Olandis, sat opposite Sean and stretched out his long legs.

'I expect you're wondering why you're here?'

'And why Krankhausen stole all my stuff?' said Sean.

'The good news is you are *not* the chosen one,' said Olandis. 'We'll leave all those fanciful notions to the movies, shall we?'

Sean laughed.

'But you are very special to us, Sean. So please be careful.'

'I will.'

'And learn to trust your instincts. It is surprising how often they can bear fruit.'

Sean looked puzzled.

'We will bring Mr Von Krankhausen to heel. Good day to you, Sean. Agent Rusham, take good care of this young man.'

'Will do, sir,' said Rusham, standing to attention.

And with that Olandis was gone, as quickly as he had appeared.

A receptionist approached.

'Your driver is waiting for you at the main reception.'

47

'Thanks,' said Rusham. 'Let's go, Sean. We need to get you home.' Rusham clicked her phone. 'Major? We have the 'all clear'. We'll meet you downstairs.'

****

'My house is just around the corner,' said Sean, leading the way.

Clavity squelched across the road, his shoes still sopping wet. Rusham traipsed along beside him, wearing a deep frown.

'And whose idea was it to go after Krankhausen?'

'How was I to know what would happen?' said Clavity, keeping one eye on their surroundings.

Professor Quark had banned them from using Foundation vehicles until further notice. Anyone would think Hermes had been destroyed. True, it was a little seized up and full of seawater, but surely Quark's technicians could sort it out? To cap it all, their driver had refused to take them anywhere near the house in case there was another gas explosion.

Sean hurried home. He found the pavement blocked by blue and white tape. Two policemen wearing black uniforms stood guard. Beyond them, a tunnel of blue plastic stretched from a white van on the driveway to the front door. Sean tried to dodge under the tape.

'I need you to go 'round,' said one of the policemen.

The second policeman noticed Clavity and looked bashful.

'Don't worry about him, Major. He's new.'

Clavity gave a half-hearted smile and made a point of showing them his identity badge.

'Sorry, sir, just doing my job.'

'Quite right too. This *is* a lock-down, gentlemen. And lay off the policeman shtick. We don't want to get caught, do we?'

The first guard winked.

'We'll keep it low key, sir.'

The second guard smiled.

48

'How was your fishing trip, sir? I heard you caught a shark?'

'Careful, sunny or I'll arrange an introduction.'

The guards laughed and stood to one side.

As he passed the van, Clavity peered inside and waved at an agent. Anxious not to miss anything, Sean craned his neck around the van's open door. When he saw what was inside, his eyes nearly popped out of his head. The van was full of tools, lights and electronic equipment. A large, insect-like creature scuttled across the floor towards him. It had the appearance of a giant, mechanical beetle with antennae and six legs. It whirred for a few seconds and stopped short of the door.

'Can I have a go?' said Sean.

'Agent Lee, I have the results you were waiting for,' said Brown, speaking into his neckpiece. 'And we have visitors. Hi, Major. And you must be Sean?'

Lee joined them, wearing a concerned look.

'Where's Mum?' said Sean.

'She's uh, resting. I'll wake her in a little while,' said Lee, 'She was...overexcited.'

Sean felt a hand on his shoulder. It was Clavity.

'Are you serious? I hope you have a good explanation?'

'She's a very determined lady,' said Lee. 'Anyway, we've made progress with our investigations.'

'Yes, we heard at HQ,' said Rusham.

Sean approached Agent Lee and drew her gaze.

'So why *did* Krankhausen steal my stuff?'

'We don't know,' said Lee. 'We're not even sure what he took.'

'A Dreampad, a pile of comics and half my house,' said a voice behind them.

'Mum!' said Sean, rushing towards her.

Mrs Yeager was groggy and needed help to stand. To Sean's relief, she appeared calm.

'Where have you been, Sean? I've been worried sick.'

Sean felt embarrassed but allowed himself to be hugged.

'We went after Krankhausen. He tried to blow us up, and we were attacked by a ferry and a shark. Eventually, a giant aircraft lifted us out of the sea. And I stayed at the Foundation's Headquarters last night. It was great.'

Mrs Yeager glared at Clavity.

'Our investigations will continue, Mrs Yeager,' said Clavity, still squelching in his shoes. 'We were quite safe. The recovery team arrived in next to no time.'

She gave Clavity a scowl that would wilt flowers at a hundred paces.

'Recovery team? Sharks?'

'Sorry,' said Clavity, squirming.

'Did you find your phone, Mum?' said Sean.

'No, but I remember answering it when I was tidying your room this morning. Or was it yesterday morning?'

'Perhaps you left it on my bed?' said Sean.

'It's possible I suppose.'

Rusham stepped forwards.

'This could be important, Mrs Yeager. Can you please give me your phone number?'

Mrs Yeager dictated, and Rusham tapped the number into her smartphone.

While Mrs Yeager caught up with Sean's news, Rusham took Clavity to one side.

'With any luck, Krankhausen stole the phone as well and we can trace its signal.'

Clavity's eyes lit up. He tried to contact Cuthbertson but found his number was engaged.

'Confounded lock-down!'

****

Professor Quark knocked twice, before bursting into Cuthbertson's private office. He closed the door behind him and surveyed the room as if expecting to find ninja warriors hiding in the corners. There were none.

'Professor, how can I help you?' said Cuthbertson, looking up from his paperwork.

Quark took a pen from Cuthbertson's desk and wrote a question on a notepad.

'Have you swept for bugs?'

Cuthbertson nodded.

'Good,' said Quark 'I have a lot to tell you. We need to arrest Jenkins and put him in an isolation cell immediately.'

'But why? He's our security expert.'

Jenkins had been working for the Foundation for as long as anyone could remember. He was a trusted and reliable member of staff.

'He's also a mole,' said Quark. 'And I have the proof right here.'

Cuthbertson shook his head while Quark showed him a report of Jenkins' activities. It became clear that Jenkins had stolen a Matteract by forging three signatures, including Cuthbertson's and Quark's. He had accessed computer files he was not authorised to see and had sent data outside of the Foundation. Quark played Cuthbertson a recording of a phone call he had intercepted.

'As I was saying, either you send me the passcodes I've requested or you won't see your sister for a very long time. Do I make myself clear?' said a metallic voice.

'Yes, perfectly clear,' said Jenkins.

'Excellent,' said the caller.

Professor Quark stopped the recording and turned to Cuthbertson.

'According to our files, Jenkins has a sister who's been missing for several months. We believe she's being held for ransom by Krankhausen.'

Cuthbertson paused to consider this information.

'Jenkins? I can't believe it. Do we know where Krankhausen was calling from?'

'Alas no, he was careful to conceal his location as well as his voice,' said Quark. 'However, we did find a text message from Krankhausen on Jenkins' phone.'

Cuthbertson issued orders for Jenkins' arrest. Next, he asked Quark to prepare the mind-probe equipment. It would be hard on Jenkins, but what choice did they have? They needed information and they needed it fast.

'What do we know about this Sean Yeager?'

'Hardly anything,' said Quark. 'All Yeager's files are locked by the Founder himself.'

Cuthbertson tapped on his keyboard and searched for Sean Yeager's files. All he found was an address and a red label marked: 'SP1'.

'I don't understand. Why would Krankhausen break into a boy's house?' said Cuthbertson. 'It makes no sense. And if *we* can't see his records, what has Jenkins discovered about Yeager?'

'I'll see what I can find out,' said Quark, rising to leave.

'Keep me informed, Professor.'

Cuthbertson checked his mobile phone. There were a few missed calls, including one from Clavity. He was in no hurry to speak to his field agents. After all, what had they achieved? They had damaged an expensive Foundation vehicle and lost all trace of Krankhausen. A pet dog would be more useful and cheaper to keep. However, Cuthbertson was worried. He remembered the St Jacobs incident and there was no telling what Krankhausen might do. The man was clearly deranged and also highly intelligent. He studied a map on his computer showing the most recent sightings.

'Where are you hiding, Krankhausen?'

He reached for his secure phone and speed-dialled.

'Reynard? This is Cuthbertson.'

'Reynard here, sir.'

'Prepare Sigma Squad for a search mission.'

'Right away, sir. Where are we going?'

'Professor Quark will send you the coordinates. We're on the hunt for Krankhausen.'

'And when we find him, sir?'

'Take him alive if you can, but I want his activities

stopped.'

'Yes, sir, we'll do our best,' said Reynard.

'I'm sure you will. Good luck,' said Cuthbertson.

****

'This lock-down is ridiculous!' said Rusham. 'Every phone I call is either engaged or switched off. Even Control!'

'I guess that's why they call it a *lock-down*,' said Clavity.

She had a point though he had to admit. How can you run an investigation if you can't call HQ for assistance? And if no one will lend you a vehicle? Agent Lee had also refused to help. She claimed her orders were to stay put and protect the Yeagers, which sounded strangely familiar.

'Have you tried calling your sweetheart?' said Clavity.

'Look, Major, he's *not* my sweetheart. I've told you a thousand times,' said Rusham, storming off.

'The lady doth protest too much, methinks,' whispered Clavity, with a wry smile.

Rusham thumbed through her phone contacts and dialled.

'Captain Reynard? It's Elise, Elise Rusham.'

'Hello, Elise. I'm sorry, I'm busy right now.'

'Look, Captain, the thing is we've found a lead about you know who and err…'

'Careful, this is an open line.'

'Yes, I know. I was wondering if you could arrange a lift for us?'

There was a long pause, and Rusham held her breath.

'I'm afraid that's impossible, Elise. I would risk being court-martialled.'

'What if there was an agent in urgent need of medical attention?' said Rusham.

'Have you called Control?'

'I've tried, but they're not answering.'

'And you're at the Yeager's house?'

'Yes, we'll be waiting for you. Thank you, Captain.'

Reynard let out a sigh.

'I'll see what I can do, but I'm making no promises.'

Rusham realised she had to work fast. She ran into the house and found the medic. He was in the living room preparing to examine Mrs Yeager.

'Hi, I've heard you're a real hero,' said Rusham.

'I do what I can,' said the medic.

'I've been meaning to ask you, how do those knock-out devices work? They must be pretty dangerous in the wrong hands?'

'Not really,' said the medic.

He opened his case and produced a small, pen-like object. It was white with a button at one end and a round, metallic bulb at the other.

'All you do is press the tip behind the subject's ear and it sends them to sleep in an instant. It transmits a harmless, electrical pulse, which relaxes the patient's brain patterns.'

'Wow, that's amazing,' said Rusham. 'Can I have a look? Promise I'll be careful.'

The medic nodded and handed her the device.

'Where are you based? Far from here?' said Rusham.

'HQ mostly, although sometimes I'm posted to the Beach-hut or the Farmstead.'

'Must be interesting?' said Rusham. 'Travelling all over the world?'

She examined the device for a few moments and pretended to drop it back into the case. If the medic had been watching more closely, he would have noticed Rusham distract his gaze at the critical moment and drop a coin in its place.

'It has its moments,' said the medic.

'Oh, by the way, Mrs Yeager is still a bit wobbly. I think Agent Lee is worried.'

'Excuse me,' said the medic, picking up his case and hurrying to find them.

Rusham returned outside. She found Clavity examining a holographic reading of footprints.

'Major, have you seen Sean recently?'

'Yes, he's in the van. Why?'

'I think I've found us a lift.'

'With anyone I know?'

Rusham gave a faint smile.

'Sean's been looking pale since we brought him home, don't you think?'

'Has the medic checked him over?' said Clavity.

'I've asked him to, but he seems to have his hands full with Mrs Yeager. Besides, it could be something serious.'

Clavity grinned.

'Are you suggesting he needs to be airlifted to a hospital by any chance, Agent Rusham?'

'It might be a good idea, sir. In the circumstances.'

'I like your thinking,' said Clavity, gesturing towards the driveway.

Inside the van, Sean was busy taking a spy-bot apart piece by piece. He followed removed a power cell from its casing.

'Well done, Sean. Good job,' said Brown.

Brown took the casing and held it up to a bench lamp. He tipped it back and forth to catch the light. As he did so, a layer of dark, metallic dust rolled around inside the plastic shell.

'Hi, Sean,' said Rusham. 'Have you figured it out yet?'

'Not quite.'

Brown looked up over his illuminated glasses.

'Their transformers were shorted out. It was probably caused by a power surge or an electromagnetic pulse.'

Clavity joined them and studied Sean's face.

'Hey, big guy, are you feeling okay? You're looking a bit pale.'

'You do look a bit hot, Sean,' said Rusham, touching Sean's brow. 'Major, what do you think?'

Clavity dabbed his hand on Sean's forehead. At the same time, Rusham reached behind Clavity's neck and tapped the sleep inducer behind his ear. Clavity gave a brief murmur and slumped to one side, relaxed and asleep.

'Major? Major!' said Rusham, hiding the sleep inducer in her pocket.

'What's the matter?' said Brown.

'Major Clavity's collapsed!'

Brown helped to carry Clavity to the front of the van and laid him on a long, cushioned seat.

'Better fetch the medic,' said Brown. 'I'll see if I can reach Control, he might need an airlift.'

'Right away,' said Rusham, putting on her serious face.

A few minutes later, the medic appeared and examined Clavity. While he did so, Rusham edged closer and dropped the sleep inducer back into his case.

'He just fainted,' said Rusham.

The medic shook his head and took Clavity's pulse.

'I spoke to Captain Reynard,' said Rusham. 'He suggested we airlift Clavity to a hospital.'

'That's probably a good idea,' said the medic. 'It could be a virus or a bug of some kind. At his age, it's best not to take any chances.'

'Huh?' said Clavity, dribbling and half awake.

Several minutes later, a large shape covered the house in shadow. Shimmering, almost invisible against the sky, it hovered over the roof, making a loud whining sound. A door opened in mid-air, and two figures appeared wearing blue and grey camouflage.

Rusham's phone rang. It was Reynard.

'We need you to clear the front lawn so we can lower a stretcher.'

'Will do,' said Rusham, waving people towards the house. A bright-orange, plastic stretcher fell from the sky. It bounced on a pair of cables and came to rest on the grass. The medic stepped forwards and set to work adjusting its harnesses, while Brown and another agent helped Clavity from the van.

'There's no way I'm going anywhere in that!' said Mrs Yeager, from the doorway.

'It's not for you. It's for Major Clavity,' said Lee.

Meanwhile, Clavity staggered towards the stretcher.

'I am *not* an invalid,' he said, almost collapsing on the lawn. 'I *can* walk you know?'

Rusham called Reynard.

'Do you have any harnesses?'

A figure high above gave a thumbs-up, and two bright orange, padded straps fell to the ground. Brown and the medic helped Clavity to secure one around his body and signalled to the waiting aircraft.

While Clavity was being winched skywards, Sean hurried to the van. He picked up a repaired spy-bot and taped two aerosol cans to its shell, so they dangled behind its legs. He carried the spy-bot to the far side of the plastic tunnel and activated it by following Brown's instructions. At once, the mechanical insect whirred and clattered its way across the driveway, dragging the cans and making an almighty din.

Sean heard startled voices and sprinted back to the van. By now, Agent Rusham was in mid-air and the lawn was deserted. He crept to the discarded stretcher, strapped himself in and hid under an orange blanket.

'Don't leave without me,' he whispered and crossed his fingers for luck.

Sure enough, after a few seconds, the stretcher became airborne. From under his blanket, he watched inquisitive faces appear at a neighbours' window and was tempted to wave back. The stretcher swayed above the rooftops, and Sean laughed at a pair of startled birds as they flew past. Eventually, he reached an opening in the sky, and the stretcher was hauled inside a cargo bay. Sean lay concealed under the blanket and waited. Before long, a hatch slammed shut and, with a thunderous roar, the Skyraptor powered away across the sky.

CHAPTER 8: HUNTING NEEDLES

Sean peered into the gloom. A solitary bulb bathed the cargo bay in pale, yellow light, and there was an acrid smell of metal and oil. When his eyes had adjusted, he noticed the walls were made of metal ribs covered in grey padding, pipes, and wires. Everything around him rattled and shook like a tumble dryer. He rose from the stretcher and hid behind some cargo boxes lashed to the floor.

'How's our patient?' said a uniformed figure, in a raised voice.

'Major Clavity seems fine to me,' said another, wearing a serpent and stick badge on his sleeve. 'I don't know why we're taking him to hospital.'

Rusham helped Clavity up a metal staircase to the flight deck. Reynard waved them into a cabin and slid a door closed, blocking out most of the noise. Inside the room was a large surface covered by holographic maps. A uniformed navigator studied a wall of screens.

'What do you have to tell me?' said Reynard.

Rusham helped Clavity to a seat before answering.

'We have the number of a mobile phone we believe Krankhausen may have stolen.'

Reynard stared at Rusham for a moment, as if waiting for more information. When none was offered, he burst into laughter.

'A phone number? Is that all? Here, let me show you something.'

He led them to the holographic maps and pointed at a vast area of pale blue. A wide scattering of dots stretched around a floating label which said: 'Hermes'. Beside it, lay a collection of numbered satellite pictures.

'You see this? We have thousands of square miles of

ocean to search and only six aircraft,' said Reynard.

Rusham nodded.

'We have hundreds of targets to investigate, and every one of them is moving. Now, do you see a single phone mast on this map?'

'But what about satellites?' said Rusham, 'I thought you could phone anywhere these days?'

'Sure, if Krankhausen has a satellite uplink *just* to answer this phone of yours,' said Reynard.

Rusham sighed and looked up at the ceiling. She felt frustrated and humiliated. But there was still a nagging question eating away inside her.

'We will take Major Clavity to a hospital and continue our search,' said Reynard.

'You see the thing is…' said Rusham, pausing to choose her words.

Reynard waited in silence as if daring Rusham to finish her sentence. During the stand-off, the navigator approached.

'Yes, Sebastian?' said Reynard.

'If the phone *is* on, we can locate its signal using two of our transmitters, sir.'

'And do we have suitable transmitters?'

'Yes, sir, all Skyraptors can send and receive mobile phone signals. But we'll need the right software to mimic the phone's cell network.'

Reynard paced the room for a few moments, deep in thought. He surveyed the holographic maps and eyed Rusham with a look of amused respect.

'Sebastian, call Control and ask them for help.'

'You'll need this,' said Rusham, proudly displaying a phone number on her smartphone.

Reynard's neckpiece beeped. He answered it and grinned at Clavity.

'It seems, Major, you have made a miraculous recovery?'

'We were just being cautious,' said Rusham.

'Tell me more, Agent Rusham.'

Before she could reply, a voice crackled on a nearby

speaker.

'It's Recon-one, sir,' said Sebastian.

'Patch them through,' said Reynard.

'Go ahead, Recon-one.'

'We have visual contact with Tango-one-niner. It's a cargo ship, over.'

'Roger that, Recon-one, proceed to Tango-two-zero,' said Sebastian.

The navigator tapped the report into a keyboard, and one of the hundreds of shapes on the main hologram changed from blue to green. He waited for a response, but there was only static.

'Recon-one, this is Sunbeam, do you copy?'

Again there was no reply. Seconds later, the speaker burst into life.

'Mayday! Mayday! This is Recon-one. We are under attack. Repeat, we are under attack!'

There was shocked silence in the room.

'Recon-one, this is Sunbeam, what is attacking you?' said Reynard.

But there was no reply.

'Where are they?' said Reynard.

'About here, sir,' said Sebastian, indicating a flashing red shape on one of the maps.

The shape hovered over deep water, miles from shore.

'Change our heading, we're going to assist,' said Reynard. 'I'll be on the flight deck. Strap in everyone, this could be a bumpy ride.'

The flight crew were tense. No one could understand how a Foundation aircraft had been seen, let alone shot down. Reynard ordered Skyraptor-one's cloaking and stealth devices to be activated as a precaution. They should be invisible to enemy radar but then so should every other Foundation aircraft.

Clavity felt better and teetered away in search of a restroom. He found one on the cargo deck and reached for its door handle. As he did so, the door slid open to reveal Sean with a look of horror on his face.

'What are *you* doing here?' said Clavity.

Sean blushed.

'Going after Krankhausen. Isn't that the plan?'

Clavity shook his head.

'Yeah, but first I need a leak. May I?'

Reynard gazed out at the ocean. He sat behind the pilot and co-pilot, who he called Flight; and beside the radar operator, who he called Radar. In front of him, a tactical screen showed possible targets on a circular grid. It displayed a red blip where Recon-one had been.

'Sunbeam, this is Control. Recon-one is heading back to base. We believe their transmitter malfunctioned, over.'

'Roger that, Control. Request permission to engage Tango-one-niner, over.'

'This is Brigadier Cuthbertson. You have permission to disable Tango One Nine but only if fired upon, over.'

'Understood, Brigadier,' said Reynard, rubbing his hands together.

Clavity led Sean to the navigation room.

'Look who I've found.'

'Sean? What are you doing here?' said Rusham.

The room was filled by radio noise, and the navigator clenched his fist.

'What's going on?' said Sean.

'We're going after a hostile ship,' said Rusham.

'With Sean on board?' said Clavity.

Rusham and Clavity exchanged bemused looks.

'Captain Reynard is in charge now,' said Rusham, in a carefree tone.

'And I'm sure you'll both be very happy,' said Clavity, winking.

Rusham scowled.

'I got us a lift, didn't I?'

The holographic map flashed a spherical target enclosed by a shape resembling a red cross-hair.

'Time to strap in, Sean,' said Clavity, indicating a spare seat. 'We're going fishing again.'

'I hope you know what you're doing this time?'

Rusham gave a broad grin.

'Care to comment, Major?'

'Don't ask me,' said Clavity, 'I'm only a passenger.'

Sean laughed.

Moments later, alarms rang out across the flight deck, and a grey and white ship appeared on the horizon.

'Captain, we have missiles locked onto us and in flight,' said Radar.

'Impossible!' said Reynard. 'We're fully cloaked.'

'Tracking two missiles. Estimated impact in thirty seconds, Captain, cloaked or otherwise.'

'Weapons, activate lasers and counter-measures,' said Reynard. 'Comms, jam their signals. Flight, take evasive action!'

Skyraptor-one climbed and turned sharply left. Its engines flared with afterburners. As it accelerated, its wings swept back and carved vapour trails through the air.

'Impact in twenty seconds,' said Radar, straining against the g-force.

'Lasers are locked on and firing,' said Weapons.

Two missiles changed direction and raced after them. Skyraptor-one fled straight up, its laser turrets flashing beams of red light in its wake. The first beam struck the nose cone of a missile and made it explode. The second missed its target and boiled sea water far below.

'We still have a missile on our tail!' said Radar.

'Counter-measures away,' said Flight.

Skyraptor-one shed a cloud of tiny, metal pieces on silver parachutes. As they fell, they exploded one by one, like fireworks. The second missile sped into the debris.

'Boom!'

'Both missiles have been destroyed,' said Radar.

'Okay, let's find the hostile ship,' said Reynard.

'Levelling out, sir,' said Flight.

Two miles above the sea, Skyraptor-one slowed and adjusted its wings. It cruised above the clouds and scanned the ocean for the enemy.

'We have contact with Tango-one-niner,' said Radar.

Reynard considered his options. He knew it would be easy to destroy a cargo ship, but how should they disable it? A missile or laser strike would make the whole ship explode, particularly if it was carrying missiles. Reynard ruled out any direct attack.

'Prepare two EMP mines for a medium-distance ignition.'

'Yes, sir,' said Weapons.

'Flight, plot a course to intercept and prepare for a high-speed bombing run.'

'Yes, sir.'

Skyraptor-one descended and approached its target in a wide circle. Ten nautical miles from the cargo ship, it dipped below the clouds and accelerated to supersonic speed.

'We have a contact,' said Radar. 'The target is confirmed as Tango-one-niner.'

'We are locked-on, sir,' said Weapons.

'Launch EMP mines when ready,' said Reynard.

'Launch ready, sir.'

'Carry on, Weapons,' said Reynard.

Before the cargo ship could sound an alarm, Skyraptor-one had flown past. Two guided bombs struck the surface of the ocean on either side of the ship. They exploded in small mushroom clouds and sent shock waves rippling in every direction. The blasts of radiation reached the cargo ship and sent electricity sparking through every piece of metal on board. Radars, missiles and transmitters blew their circuit boards. Computers overloaded and shut down. And all the lights went out. The cargo ship slowed and began to drift on the waves, miles from anywhere.

'Tango-one-niner is damaged, sir. It's lost all power,' said Radar.

'Good work, team,' said Reynard. 'Comms, report the target's location and status to HQ.'

'Will do, sir.'

'Perhaps Cuthbertson himself will pay them a visit?' said Reynard, barely disguising a grin.

CHAPTER 9: DAMAGE

The Control Centre buzzed with activity. Screens flashed and keyboards were pounded as Foundation agents did their best to find Krankhausen. Reports flooded in from aircraft of all shapes and sizes, filling the room with radio chatter. Professor Quark climbed a short flight of steps to the inner sanctum.

'Brigadier, I have grave news.'

'What is it, Professor?'

'I've been reviewing the findings from Jenkins' mind probe sessions. We found evidence that he's been leaking secrets to Krankhausen for months. We also found some strange puncture marks on the back of his neck.'

Cuthbertson groaned. This was worse than he feared. He had never really liked Jenkins, because of his slicked-back hair and whiny manner. However, he had a begrudging respect for the man because of his in-depth knowledge of security matters.

'Jenkins also managed to ship a number of Foundation weapons abroad disguised as machine parts.'

'Do we know what they were?' said Cuthbertson.

Quark puffed out his cheeks.

'They could have been almost anything. Jenkins even had access to our secret research projects.'

Cuthbertson stared at the ceiling. A minor burglary had turned into a crisis. Recon-one was limping back to base, the enemy missile ship had somehow vanished, and Reynard was hunting an invisible madman. To make matters worse, Krankhausen was armed to the teeth with the Foundation's own weapons.

'What about this Sean Yeager? Have you managed to find out why he's a priority-one subject?' said Cuthbertson.

Quark wiped his glasses before answering.

'All his files are locked and encrypted. However, the Founder books him a medical every year.'

'We all have medicals,' said Cuthbertson.

'Of course, but you should see the list of procedures. Sean has every scan, measurement, and test I've ever heard of and plenty more besides.'

'I don't understand,' said Cuthbertson. 'Why would the Founder be interested in Yeager's health?'

'I wonder,' said Quark. 'Perhaps he's Sean's guardian?'

Cuthbertson paled. It was beginning to come back to him now. Mrs Yeager had lost her partner during a Foundation mission, and the Founder had promised to protect her for life. In effect, the Founder *was* looking after the boy. Cuthbertson rose and addressed everyone in the Control Centre.

'Can anyone tell me where Sean Yeager is right now?'

Every agent in the room studied their screen and pretended to be busy. Cuthbertson glanced at Quark, who gave a pained expression.

'No! Don't tell me he's with...'

Quark gave a pained look.

'Get me Reynard this instant!'

****

Egbert Von Krankhausen prowled the main deck of his base. It was an impressive structure sat in the middle of the ocean. He watched the horizon through an expanse of tinted glass. The main deck was a large and comfortable space containing plants, sofas, and an impressive array of hi-tech equipment. On one side of the room, a row of technicians worked a bank of screens. Greerbo stood behind them, offering snarls of encouragement, like a sheepdog keeping watch over its flock.

'Where are they, Greerbo?' said Krankhausen. 'I want to see them explode in front of me.'

'They've evaded our missile ships, boss.'

'Pah! Enough of these games! Launch the Paladins.'

'You heard the man!' said Greerbo.

The white coats scurried into action and lit up another row of consoles.

'Boss, what shall I do with Jenkins?'

Krankhausen's lips curled into a narrow smile, and he stroked his bearded chin.

'Trigger his implants. Jenkins could become a most valuable asset.'

****

Sean was bored and tapped his feet against the metal floor. Skyraptor-one had been circling for ages, and there was still no sign of Krankhausen. He listened to the reports as they came in. Foundation patrols had identified cruise liners, ferries, cargo ships, and pleasure boats but nothing suspicious. If Krankhausen was out there, he was well hidden.

'Sean, shall we take a look at the flight deck?' said Clavity.

'Can we?' said Sean, excitedly.

'I'm coming with you,' said Rusham.

The three passengers staggered down a narrow corridor. Clavity reached a bulkhead door and heaved it open to reveal sunlight and a hive of activity. An expanse of switches and equipment stretched out before them. Thousands of lights flickered and dozens of screens flashed. Beyond them, Sean noticed a perfect blue sky resting on a carpet of fluffy, white clouds.

'Hi, I'd forgotten you were on board,' said Reynard, spinning around in his chair. 'And who is this? What are *you* doing on board?''

Sean offered his hand.

'Sean Yeager, pleased to meet you.'

'Pleased to meet you, young man,' said Reynard, shaking his hand. 'And what you do you think of our flight deck?'

'It's amazing!' said Sean, his eyes wide.

Reynard studied him with a look of suspicion.

'Any sign of Krankhausen?' said Clavity. 'We must be running low on fuel by now?'

Reynard glanced at a nearby screen and smiled.

'Major, we have enough fuel to run our micro-fusion engines for days. However, Krankhausen still eludes us.'

Sean closed his eyes and began to shake.

'What is it, Sean? Are you okay?' said Rusham

'We need to get anyway from here.'

'Why? There's nothing but sky and clouds up here,' said Rusham.

Sean's face drained of colour.

'Something terrible's coming,' he said.

'What do you mean?'

'They're angry. Really angry.'

A nearby member of crew flicked a switch and answered a call.

'Captain, it's HQ. Brigadier Cuthbertson wants to speak to you urgently.'

'Go ahead, Control,' said Reynard, turning his chair. He took the call and span around with a grave expression.

'Major, we are to return Sean Yeager to HQ at once. The Brigadier is very upset.'

Clavity frowned.

'But surely he's in safe hands now?'

'And what about the phone?' said Rusham.

An orange light flashed, and two blips appeared on a tracking screen.

'Captain, we have two incoming contacts.'

'What's their heading?' said Reynard.

'They're coming straight at us,' said Radar 'No, they can't be!'

'What is it?' said Reynard.

'The contacts are travelling at Mach 5, sir.'

The tracking screen went blank. Radar tapped a few controls and shook her head.

'Control, this is Sunbeam, please confirm our satellite-link is working?'

'Sunbeam, this is Control, we've lost you on our tracking systems. Take extreme caution, over.'

'Is there a problem?' said Reynard.

Before Radar could reply, a booming voice rattled the speakers.

'This is Cuthbertson, leave the area immediately. Repeat, leave the…'

Cuthbertson's voice trailed off into static.

'What's happening, Comms?' said Reynard.

'We've lost contact with Control, sir.'

Reynard pulled a face and tapped commands into his own screen.

There was a huge roar outside, and two objects raced by. They sped into the distance, becoming tiny dots in next to no time. Just as quickly, the specks returned, and there was a brilliant flash as they roared past.

'What was that?' said Reynard.

'We've been hit, sir!' said Flight. 'On our starboard wing.'

'I can't see anything on radar, sir.'

'Our defences are active,' said Weapons. 'But we can't seem to lock onto them.'

'Flight, get us into the clouds!' said Reynard. 'We're sitting ducks up here!'

At once, the deck sloped forwards.

'Grab hold of something!' said Rusham

Sean scrambled for an empty seat and groaned as he knocked his hip against a metal edge. The Skyraptor continued to dive, and Sean became stuck against a map table, barely able to breathe. Rusham dragged him across the deck floor. Together, they leaned against a metal panel and strained against the pull of gravity. Meanwhile, Clavity flew headlong into the rear of Reynard's seat and struck his head. Sean turned and saw blood trickling from his forehead. Clavity's head slumped forwards.

Skyraptor-one levelled out inside a bank of dense cloud and slowed down. There were more roars as the enemy aircraft raced past but no more flashes.

'Damage report?' said Reynard.

'All systems are operational, sir. Micro-bots are repairing the damage to our wing,' said Flight.

'I've never seen anyone fly so fast. Any ideas?' said Reynard.

Sean picked himself up and joined Rusham, who was kneeling beside Clavity.

'There's no one on those planes,' said Sean, within earshot of Reynard.

'Impossible!' said Reynard. 'They *must* have pilots.'

'I'm not picking up any life-signs,' said Radar.

'He could be right, sir,' said Flight. 'We were testing a high-speed stealth drone at the Farmstead only last spring.'

'What?' said Reynard. 'Why wasn't I informed?'

'It was a classified project, sir,' said Flight.

Reynard let out a snort of disdain.

'And if they *are* drones, how do we stop them? Or is that classified too?'

'We need to jam their control signals,' said Radar. 'They're like remote control toys, only bigger and faster.'

'Were you at the Farmstead as well?' said Reynard.

'Not as such,' said Radar, blushing.

'Okay, let's do it. Weapons, can you shoot them down?'

'Not in this fog, sir. It's blocking our targeting systems.'

'Ready to scan for the bandits' control signal, sir,' said Radar.

'Meaning?'

'We need them to buzz past us again so we can detect their signals.'

'Mer…credi!' said Reynard. 'We have to offer ourselves to these wolves like a helpless lamb?'

'It's the only way, sir,' said Radar.

While Reynard made his decision, Rusham tended to Clavity's wound using a first aid pack. He was awake but shaken, and his forehead needed stitches. Rusham put a field dressing over his eye and did her best to clean his face. Sean helped by passing sterile wipes and cotton wool swabs.

'Right,' said Reynard, 'let's stop these drones.'

Sean realised Reynard was angry and trembled at the thought of confronting the drones. He felt his stomach churn.

'Weapons, prepare heat-seeking missiles. Flight, I want to be skimming the clouds, no higher,' said Reynard.

Skyraptor-one rose out of the fog and waited. A loud roar announced the return of the drones. They streaked overhead from tail to nose, firing as they went. Once they had passed, there were bursts of flames from underneath the Skyraptor, and two missiles raced after them.

'I have their frequencies,' said Radar. 'Jamming the drone's control signals now.'

The drones turned and sped back towards them. The first flew straight into the path of a pursuing missile and exploded into thousands of pieces. However, the second continued on a collision course.

'It's going to hit us!' said Flight, dipping Skyraptor-one's nose at the last second.

The drone thundered past, missing them by the smallest of margins and flew on in a straight line. A third missile followed its wake.

'Missile in flight and locked-on,' said Weapons. 'Contact in…a few minutes.'

'Minutes?' said Reynard.

'We've lost it. The target is out of range, sir,' said Radar.

'Our missile is self-destructing,' said Weapons.

'Daileeshphi!' said Reynard, slamming his fist against the chair.

Rusham gave a surprised look.

'Temper, temper,' she whispered.

****

Jenkins woke in a cell at Foundation HQ. He wore a one-piece overall and discovered his glasses and personal effects were missing. He remembered feeling uneasy and being wheeled into a room resembling an operating theatre. He had no idea what had happened afterwards. Perhaps he had dreamt the whole thing? But that would not explain his predicament.

He walked across the cell and began to feel anxious. His head span with strange images, and his heart beat wildly. In his mind's eye, he saw pictures of a house on fire. It was his sister's house. There were weapons being fired, and the house erupted in flames. It was Cuthbertson's fault he reasoned, who else could have ordered these things? Jenkins began to shake with anger. He felt a surge of hatred build inside him and staggered to his meagre bed. His body throbbed, and his vision blurred red.

'You'll pay for what you've done,' he snarled, and keeled over onto the mattress, shaking.

Greaves was passing by and heard Jenkins moaning. He squinted through an eyeglass in the cell door and was alarmed by what he saw. The prisoner was curled up on his bed, shaking from head to toe. His face was flushed, and his mouth was wide open. Jenkins clawed at the air above him as if trying to fight off an unseen attacker. Greaves pressed a panic button on the wall and spoke into his neckpiece.

'Pearson! Craddock! Call the medics; Jenkins is having a fit! And suit up; you're coming in with me.'

He set his baton to stun and went in search of a helmet and protective collar. These crazies were capable of anything; he'd seen it all before. His colleagues arrived in full riot gear, eager for a scrap.

'Pearson, fetch the cradle. We're going to strap him in and wheel him to the sick bay, understood?'

'Yes, sir.'

Greaves opened the cell door and edged towards the prisoner. Jenkins seemed unaware of his presence and continued to battle his invisible demons. In the meantime, Pearson wheeled in the restraining cradle. Greaves pointed at Jenkins' legs, following a drill they had practiced a hundred times before. Pearson and Craddock gave a thumbs-up. They inched closer and pounced, each grabbing an ankle. Greaves stood beside Jenkins, ready to zap him unconscious at the first sign of trouble.

However, Jenkins had other ideas. He kicked both legs upwards and knocked Pearson and Craddock flying into the wall. In one movement, he arched his back like a gymnast and rose into a handstand. Greaves caught him with a glancing bolt of electricity, but it had little effect. Jenkins tumbled head over heels and twisted in the air. In a panic, Greaves aimed for his neck but missed. Now Jenkins was upon him. He struck Greaves firmly in the stomach and made him double-up on the floor, before wrenching the baton from his grasp.

By this time, Pearson and Craddock had recovered their senses and blocked Jenkins' path to the door. They drew batons of their own and stood, shoulder to shoulder, ready for a scrap. Jenkins let out a snarl and charged at them, hurling his weapon. It sparked and struck Craddock squarely in the chest, a fraction of a second before Jenkins himself arrived. Craddock was bowled over like an electrocuted skittle and lay inert on the floor. Pearson grabbed Jenkins by the arm and had his legs swept out from underneath him. He rolled and fired at Jenkins' head but only succeeded in melting a ceiling light and plunging the cell into darkness.

Greaves struggled to his feet in time to see Jenkins sprint away down the corridor, cackling at his regained freedom. Greaves activated his neckpiece.

'Control? We have a prisoner on the loose. Lock down the cell block, and seal the guardroom.'

There was a muffled sound of laughter.

'Have you been jumped again, Greaves?' said Control.

'Knock it off, will you? The prisoner is armed and dangerous, approach with extreme caution.'

'Do you need help?'

Greaves watched Pearson and Craddock struggle to their feet. He was sorely tempted to agree.

'No, it's nothing we can't handle,' he replied and switched

off his transmitter.

'I bet he's heading for the armoury,' said Pearson.

CHAPTER 10: GAMBLE

Greerbo was in a foul mood and stabbed at the controls of his drone in frustration. An enemy aircraft was at his mercy, and all he had to do was fire. He moved in for the kill and squeezed the trigger. He expected the Paladin's laser cannons to flash in front of him, but nothing happened.

'Who's been meddling with my controls?' They should be in pieces by now!'

Beside him, a frightened technician studied a screen and shook her head in disbelief.

'There's nothing wrong. Your Paladin's in perfect condition,' she said.

'Then why won't it fire?' said Greerbo, letting out a snarl.

He wrestled the controls, but the Paladin refused to respond to any of his commands.

'Someone's jamming our signals,' said the technician.

'What? Then do something!'

Greerbo's video feed went blank, and the technician's shoulders slumped. The drone, or what was left of it, had fallen into the ocean.

'Try Paladin Two, I think it's still responding,' said the technician, backing away.

Greerbo grunted and approached the pilot of the second drone. He pushed his chair so hard, it span away across the room and struck the edge of a table. The chair tipped over and deposited the startled pilot on the floor. He was about to complain when he saw the look of thunder on Greerbo's face. Instead, he crept to a safe distance.

'Useless!' said Greerbo. 'This one's broken as well.'

'What is it, Greerbo?' asked an insistent voice.

It was Krankhausen, flanked on either side by an armed guard.

'The Paladins are failing us, boss.'

'The Paladins or our pilots?' said Krankhausen. 'I've given you the best equipment the world has to offer, and you've failed to destroy a single Foundation aircraft!'

'Guards, take him away!' said Krankhausen, pointing at the startled ex-pilot of Paladin Two.

The pilot considered running, but the guards closed in around him and drew their weapons.

'And Greerbo, I expect better from you. You must redouble your efforts. Order our missile ships to shoot down those Foundation idiots.'

'Right away, boss.'

'And I want Jenkins activated at once. His mission is to destroy the Foundation's Headquarters. He'll enjoy that; if he survives.'

'And then what?' said Greerbo.

'And then nothing. Jenkins will be of no further use to us,' said Krankhausen, with a cruel stare.

'Yes, boss,' said Greerbo. 'I won't fail you.'

'True,' said Krankhausen. 'Nobody fails me for long. Guards, show this gentleman the way out.'

The pilot struggled free of his captors and ran for an exit.

'Don't just stand there!' said Krankhausen. 'Our friend has an appointment at the bottom of the ocean.'

****

Skyraptor-one had been circling in cloud cover for some time. Its wings were spread wide, and it probed the sea and sky searching for threats. Beneath its outer skin, micro-bots repaired a damaged wing strut. It was a slow job.

'Any sign of the second drone?' said Reynard.

'Nothing, sir,' said Radar.

'Have you managed to locate the source of its control signal?'

'I've tried, sir, but they seem to be coming from hundreds of locations. Their signals are echoing across a hundred-mile radius.'

'He's down there somewhere, I can feel it in my bones.'

Reynard considered his options. Should they return to HQ or continue their search for Krankhausen? He dearly wanted to teach Krankhausen a lesson, and it would not be in French History.

'Sir, we have incoming messages from our recon craft. They request permission to return to base for re-fuelling,' said Comms.

'Permission granted,' said Reynard. 'Tell them to stay alert, in case more drones turn up.'

'Yes, sir,' said Comms, typing the message.

Sean rose from his chair and approached Reynard.

'I know where Krankhausen is,' he said.

'You do?' said Reynard, raising his eyebrows.

'He's waiting for us down there,' said Sean, pointing at the sea.

'But how can you know this, Sean?' said Reynard. 'Krankhausen is probably thousands of miles away by now.'

'I just get these feelings,' said Sean, hesitantly.

'Feelings?' said Reynard. 'But do you have any evidence?'

Rusham left her nursing duties and joined them.

'We could always try the phone?'

Reynard screwed up his face as if he had bitten into a slice of lemon.

'Alright, Agent Rusham, I give in. We will test this theory of yours.'

'Comms, contact Skyraptor-two and prepare to call this phone number,' said Reynard, smirking.

'Will do, sir. It will take about five minutes to set up the transmission.'

Reynard turned to Sean with a twinkle in his eye.

'And tell me, Master Sean, what do your feelings tell you about this plan of ours?'

Sean stared into the distance.

'It depends,' he said.

'On what?'

'On when *they* arrive.'

Reynard gave a quizzical expression.

'Our transmitters are ready, sir,' said Comms.

'Okay, call the number,' said Reynard.

'The phone is ringing, sir.'

Reynard sighed to himself. He suspected the phone had been left on a shop counter somewhere by a distracted mother. It would either ring before diverting to voicemail, or its battery would already be exhausted. No matter, at least it would keep Rusham quiet for a while. However, Sean's answer concerned him. Who were or what were *they*?

****

In an empty laboratory, Willard inspected a row of cloudy test tubes.

'What's the matter with you? Separate, damn you!'

He watched a batch of hair samples cook in a chemical soup. Meanwhile, the rest of the hair had been cleaned and stored as instructed by Krankhausen. In normal circumstances, he would have several thousand copies of DNA by now. However, this DNA had refused to be copied, and he had been forced to start again.

Willard was worried. Not about the DNA, so what if it was abnormal? He was concerned about Greerbo. That animal needed to be kept in a cage, preferably underwater. Which reminded him—he needed to feed Krankhausen's experiment, and he would have to endure that awful stench.

Willard went through a mental checklist. His equipment was all in order, but he realised he had forgotten to chill any alcohol. He clapped his hands together in frustration. How many times had he performed this procedure? He opened a cupboard and hauled out a Winchester full of ethanol. As ever, its weight caught him by surprise. He set it on a workbench and went in search of a measuring tube. As he started to pour the liquid, a strange buzzing noise and music echoed across the lab. He spilt ethanol on his fingers and cursed. It felt cold and began to evaporate, so he hurried to wash his hands under a tap. He hated the way it dried and cracked his skin.

The noise stopped, and Willard relaxed. He had just covered his hands in soap when the music began to play again. It was coming from a plastic crate in the corner of the laboratory.

'How am I expected to work in these conditions?' he growled.

Willard stomped over to the crate and rummaged around to find the source of the disturbance. He discovered a silver mobile phone, which continued to buzz and play music in his wet, soapy hand.

'Can't you see I'm busy?' he cried and threw the phone across the laboratory.

It flashed and buzzed on its short journey over a workbench. The phone struck the back of a metal chair and bounced. Turning end over end, it clattered against the edge of a centrifuge and came to rest upside down against a gas tap. It continued to ring.

'How dare you?' cried Willard.

He stormed across the room and pounded the phone with his fist. Its screen shattered, and his second blow silenced it. Willard picked up the damaged phone between two fingers and dropped it in a yellow bin labelled: 'Hazardous Waste'.

'Ha! You disgusting machine. Try disturbing me from the incinerator,' he said, stomping away to finish his work.

And then the phone clicked back into life.

****

On the flight deck of Skyraptor-one, Sean listened to a dialling tone ring and ring.

'No response, sir,' said Comms.

'Try it again,' said Reynard, glancing at Rusham.

Comms tapped instructions into a computer, and the dialling tones returned.

'Ringing now, sir.'

'Beep, beep! Beep, beep! Beep, beep!'

'As I thought,' said Reynard. 'It's not even going to voicemail.'

Sean watched Rusham and Clavity strain to hear the dialling tones. They reminded him of anxious parents at a school play. All of a sudden, there was a muffled 'click' followed by static and a distant voice.

'What was that?' said Rusham.

'It sounded like: you disgusting machine,' said Sean.

'It sounded like gold dust to me!' said Clavity.

'Do we have a fix on the phone's signal?' said Reynard.

'Yes, sir!' said two voices together.

'On display now,' said Radar.

The main screen showed an area of ocean covered by hundreds of orange dots. In the lower quarter, a solitary dot flashed green. Reynard rubbed his hands together.

'Comms, patch me through to Skyraptor-two. We have a criminal to catch.'

Clavity gave Rusham a thumbs-up, and she smiled back with her 'I told you so' look.

'This is Reynard, all crew to attack stations. Which includes you three. Come on, jump to it!'

Rusham approached Reynard's chair.

'Did you say something about phone masts?'

Reynard gave a sheepish smile.

'We can celebrate your hunch when our mission is complete.'

'Promises, promises,' said Clavity.

Sean felt a sense of dread deep inside. He knew something evil lay in the ocean and felt a pair of dark, soulless eyes watching him.

'They're waiting for us,' he whispered.

****

Jenkins discovered a storage cupboard and slipped inside.

It was full of cleaning equipment. He flicked on a light switch and discovered a cart laden with bottles, an array of mops, and cloths. He jammed the door shut using a mop handle and glanced up. In the ceiling was an air vent fronted by a metal grille. Visions again filled his head. He saw bonfires, gas stoves and flames. In his twisted mind, everything in the cupboard became a fuel.

'You had this coming, Brigadier.'

Jenkins piled rags and cloths on the floor and soaked them in cleaning fluid. The smell almost made him choke. Next, he moved the cart under the air vent and climbed up to shake the grill. It cut into his fingers and specks of blood splattered on the floor. However, Jenkins felt nothing but an unstoppable rage. Rooting around in the back of the cupboard, he found a tray of rusty tools. He selected a screwdriver and began to unfasten the grill. After a short while, it crashed to the floor. Jenkins peered into the darkness. It was a route he knew well from studying plans of the building, but would the air duct hold his weight? There was only one way to find out.

There were voices and footsteps in the corridor. The door handle rattled. Orders were barked and someone started pounding on the cupboard door. Jenkins wrapped his hand in a cloth and tugged the light fitting. The ceiling cracked, and the glass bulb smashed on the floor. The light went out, and the still glowing filament landed in a puddle of floor cleaner.

'Woof!'

A fire spread across the liquid and reached the rags. At first, they smouldered, before catching fire and filling the cupboard with smoke.

Several guards gathered in the corridor. They took turns hitting the cupboard door with anything they could find. Fire extinguishers were more effective than shoulders and feet, but still the door remained intact.

'Stand aside!' said a figure, dressed in grey and blue body armour.

It was a commando. He drew a blaster from his holster, selected a heat setting and fired. The door handle glowed orange and charred the surrounding wood. The commando picked up a discarded fire extinguisher and smashed it against the handle. At once, the lock snapped, and the door swung open. An instant later, the commando was blown off his feet by a blast of flames from inside the cupboard. He landed on his back with his feet in the air.

'Shall we use it properly this time?' said Greaves, picking up the dented fire extinguisher and pointing it at the flames.

A series of deafening fire alarms rang out and water sprinklers doused the corridor in a dense mist. While Greaves put out the fire, Jenkins crawled away through the air vent. One step closer to his target.

CHAPTER 11: ASSAULT

The Control Centre at Foundation HQ was in disarray. Its satellite links were broken and Cuthbertson had no way of contacting Reynard. There were puddles in the cellblock corridor, and acrid smoke had spread through the East Wing. The fire was out, but Jenkins was proving difficult to find. Even with video cameras, spy-bots and guards in pursuit, Jenkins eluded them. However, the fire alarms were at last silent.

Brigadier Cuthbertson accepted a phone call from Greaves.

'Let me get this straight,' said Cuthbertson. 'Jenkins has gone crazy, he's escaped into an air vent, and he's trying to burn down the building?'

'Yes, sir. We think he's heading for the armoury.'

Cuthbertson turned to Professor Quark for reassurance.

'Is there any way Jenkins can get into the armoury?'

'He would need to reach the main lift shaft,' said Quark, frowning.

The consequences of a maniac letting off weapons inside the Foundation's armoury did not bear thinking about. It held missiles, and anti-matter grenades, among other devices. An explosion would cause a chain reaction, which would wipe the building off the face of the planet.

'Greaves, find Jenkins, and use any means necessary to stop him,' said Cuthbertson.

'Right away, sir.'

Cuthbertson turned to a tall, bald-headed commando and looked him straight in the eye. The commando stood to attention.

'Captain Ayres, use your men to secure every possible entry point to the armoury. When you find Jenkins use any means necessary, but please try to take him alive.'

'Yes, sir,' said Ayres.

'Good luck.'

Ayres saluted and hurried away to organise his men.

'And what about the rest of the building?' said Quark. 'What about my laboratories?'

'Good point, Professor.'

'Control, order all agents to report for security duties.'

'I'll send the order out right away, sir,' said the Duty Officer.

****

Rusham led Clavity to Skyraptor-one's medical bay and encouraged him to lie down on a stretcher. It was a narrow space, but it was well equipped. A medic arrived and examined Clavity's wound. Around them, commandos buzzed excitedly and inspected their equipment. There had been several injuries during their recent aerobatics, and Rusham nodded in sympathy as men rubbed sore knees and elbows.

Sean enjoyed being on the flight deck because there was so much happening. Scopes bleeped and hundreds of lights blinked. He listened to the speakers and headphones around him. There was a constant chatter as the crew prepared for their mission. He discovered that Skyraptor-two was codenamed Deuce and was going to join them on their mission. The plan was to find Krankhausen's base and send in an assault team.

'Deuce, this is Sunbeam, join us on our starboard side,' said Reynard.

'Will do, Sunbeam. Our ETA is two minutes.'

'Flight, take us above the clouds,' said Reynard. 'Radar, any sign of the drone?'

'Nothing on our scanners, sir.'

'Keep looking, it must be out there somewhere.'

A few minutes later, heads turned to watch a flickering

shape outside.

'Sunbeam, this is Deuce, we are alongside you now.'

Through a cockpit window, Sean spotted the faint outline of an aircraft flying beside them. It was long and slender with four swept wings and twin angular tailfins. It looked beautiful and menacing at the same time.

'Deuce, prepare for a video link,' said Reynard, adjusting his camera.

'This is Deuce, go ahead.'

Reynard raised a hand in greeting. Sean strained to see a tiny blonde head appear on Reynard's personal screen.

'Lieutenant, glad you could join us,' said Reynard.

'I wouldn't miss it for the world, sir.'

'Funny you should say that. We don't know what Krankhausen has in store for us down there, so we're going to play it safe. We need to take him alive, much as it pains me.'

'Understood, Captain.'

'Prepare for a steep pass and stay close. We'll use aerial mines to smoke him out and re-group for the main event. Any questions?'

'No, sir, we're raring to go.'

'Good luck, Lieutenant.'

'Good luck to you, sir.'

****

Krankhausen dragged Greerbo to a large, blue scanner on the wall. It showed two red shapes approaching the centre of a rectangular grid. The shapes flashed every time the scope swept over them.

'How did they find us, Greerbo? We should be invisible to their sensors.'

'I don't know, boss.'

'Shoot them down! I don't care how. Throw everything we have at them.'

Greerbo eyed a nervous gathering of technicians.

'Yes, boss, it will be my pleasure. You heard the man, get back to work!'

****

'Crew, this is Reynard, we've located Krankhausen's base, and we're about to begin our first pass. Strap yourselves in, and prepare for a steep dive.'

In Skyraptor-one's hold, the commandos gave a loud cheer. Rusham and Clavity raised their eyebrows.

'Strange people these commandos,' whispered Clavity.

Rusham laughed.

'Stranger than your friends in the Army?'

'I don't know what you mean,' said Clavity.

Sean noticed heat shields slide across the cockpit windows, and the lights dimmed.

'Weapons, prepare smoke clusters and aerial mines,' said Reynard.

'All weapons are primed and ready to roll, sir.'

'Flight, take us in as fast as you can,' said Reynard.

'Commencing attack run in five, four, three, two, now.'

Sean felt his stomach tense and his ears pop. Skyraptor-one dived almost vertically and built up tremendous speed. There was a loud rushing sound, and in seconds they were cutting through the clouds. Faster and faster they fell, throwing Sean forwards against his straps. His cheeks shook with the g-force.

'Release mines when in range,' said Reynard.

'Mines away, sir.'

'Deuce confirms the release of their weapons,' said Comms.

Skyraptor-one banked away into a steep climb. Behind them, a cluster of mines exploded in mid-air. It was louder than any firework display Sean had ever heard. The strain on his stomach made him cry out, and the seat dug into the small of his back. He closed his eyes and wished the fairground ride would come to an end.

'Three missiles tracking us have been shot down, sir,' said Weapons.

'Deuce, are you with us?' said Reynard

'Right on your tail, Sunbeam.'

'Head for the outer marker,' said Reynard.

'Will do, Sunbeam, out.'

****

Krankhausen struggled to his feet and looked up. The glass roof had splintered like a frozen spider's web, yet somehow it held together. A deep rumble of aircraft engines faded into the distance. However, the sun and sky were blocked out by a dense fog, and not even the lower decks were visible.

'Did we hit them?' said Krankhausen, to no one in particular.

There was no reply because only a handful of technicians were left. The rest had taken their chance and escaped. Those who remained staggered back to their stations. Sparks fizzed from a row of computers and Greerbo sprayed them with a fire extinguisher. Their circuit boards were already burnt, and it didn't help that Greerbo covered them in white powder. Krankhausen seized a weapon from a fallen bodyguard and turned to his depleted crew. The guard recovered into a kneeling position and put his hands up in surrender, but Krankhausen ignored him.

'If anyone else is thinking of leaving, they'll have me to answer to!' he cried, waving the gun in the air.

The technicians froze.

'Get back to work!' said Krankhausen.

'Now!' said Greerbo.

****

Sean began to relax when Skyraptor-one settled into a

level cruise. After all the excitement, his body needed a rest. The shutters slid open, and he watched majestic clouds rise to meet them.

'Deuce, this is Sunbeam. What is your status?' said Reynard.

'We took some minor damage, but our systems are operational, over.'

'Follow us down, and prepare for a low-level missile attack,' said Reynard.

'Will do, Sunbeam, out.'

Sean braced himself for another dive, but this time they descended in a wide corkscrew, which seemed to go on forever.

'Radar, any signs of enemy activity?' said Reynard.

'No, sir, there's nothing on our scopes. I think we've knocked out their tracking systems.'

'We'll see,' said Reynard. 'Flight, begin your attack run.'

Sean watched the ocean become nearer and nearer. White flecks turned into waves and the bluish-grey surface grew into an expanse of constantly moving water.

'We're going to land in the sea!' he cried.

'Relax, Sean, they're professionals,' said Rusham.

There was a grinding, mechanical sound beneath them.

'Main weapons bay open, sir.'

'Prepare to launch targeting drones on my command,' said Reynard '3, 2, 1, launch!'

Sean heard a sound like thunder, and a fiery missile emerged ahead of them. It cruised above the sea and was joined by an identical twin on a parallel course. The two craft accelerated away and vanished into the distance. On the horizon, a cloud of red smoke hung in the air. From within the smoke, flashes of red light shone erratically in all directions.

'Flight, increase our altitude for weapons launch,' said Reynard.

Sean flinched as they rose once more.

'Weapons, launch Hammerheads and climb to observation

height,' said Reynard.

A whining sound of hydraulic motors was followed by another loud roar. Skyraptor-one banked to the right and increased its speed.

****

Krankhausen sensed the red fog was beginning to lift and raised his binoculars. In the distance, he noticed two grey dots approach. His defences tried to lock onto them and fired laser beams into the sky, but every shot was wayward. He realised the targeting system was damaged and cursed in frustration. The dots grew into tiny aircraft and flew ever closer. Gatling guns pounded the sky with lead, but the aircraft divided and increased their speed.

'It'll take more than two missiles to scare me!' said Krankhausen.

For a split-second, he saw a flicker of a blue and grey aircraft in the distance. Two stubby cylinders fell from out of nowhere. They split apart and dropped countless needle-like shapes towards the sea. Every needle sprouted flames and began to race towards them. Krankhausen shivered.

'Greerbo, lower the Orca! We're leaving!'

Chaos broke out on the main deck. The remaining guards and technicians ran for their lives. Krankhausen fired warning shots into the ceiling but only succeeded in making them run faster. Moments later, the first missiles struck and shook the platform like an earthquake. A laser turret exploded below them, followed by another and another. The fragile roof shattered into millions of shards of glass. Technicians and guards dived for cover wherever they could find it. Some took refuge under tables or equipment racks, while others reached stairwells and went in search of life rafts on the lower decks.

Krankhausen tucked his head under his arms and ran for an exit pursued by Greerbo. They had almost reached the stairs when they were thrown off their feet by another wave of explosions. The platform lurched to one side, and the deck shook as numerous missiles reached their targets. Beneath them, girders groaned, and a whole section of living quarters fell into the sea. Yet somehow the main deck remained intact. When it seemed the worst was over, a tower high above them creaked. It fell with an almighty crash and flattened one side of the platform like cardboard. Greerbo helped Krankhausen to his feet, and together they limped to the stairs.

****

Sean felt Skyraptor-one slow to a crawl and spotted a column of black smoke streaming from a damaged structure in the distance. It resembled an elaborate oilrig and had concentric rings of rounded decks and turrets. One side had collapsed, and the twisted girders of a tower leaned at a sharp angle towards the sea.

'What's happening?' said Sean.

Clavity peered out of the window and clenched his fist.

'We've got him!'

But Sean was distracted. A vision of swirling water filled his mind, and he slumped back in his seat.

'Sean, what's the matter?' said Rusham.

'Someone's coming.'

'Who?' said Clavity.

'I don't know, but they're angry. They want revenge.'

Meanwhile, a murmur of happy voices spread across the flight deck.

'Flight, prepare to recover our targeting drone,' said Reynard.

'Slowing to hover speed, sir.'

'Targeting drone approaching, ETA three minutes,' said Weapons.

'Deuce, prepare your assault teams for deployment,' said Reynard.

'Will do, Sunbeam. We are recovering our targeting drone and will deploy shortly.'

****

Jenkins thumped a vent cover until it fell open on its hinges. He craned his neck to scan the room below and was relieved to find it empty. He crawled forwards, squeezed his hips through the opening and dropped to the floor with a thump. His bare feet landed heavily on a hard floor, but he felt almost nothing. Nor did he notice a fresh graze on his stomach. He crouched and looked around. The office was bare and contained a desk, a chair, and a bookshelf but little else. There was an outside window and a glass panel beside an interior door. In most respects, it was identical to his old office. He even remembered visiting the room for meetings. But that was before Cuthbertson had betrayed him. And before his sister had been attacked in her own home. He snarled at the memories.

Jenkins realised he was only three floors above the armoury. All he needed was to gain access to a secure lift at the end of the corridor. He scoured the room for weapons and tools, but all he could find was furniture and a metal coat stand. He decided to improvise.

Again, visions of fire and destruction filled his troubled mind. When would they leave him in peace? He remembered his poor, twin sister and vowed Cuthbertson would pay a dear price for what he had done to her.

CHAPTER 12: DESCENT

Clavity felt restless. The medic had stitched up his cut, and his forehead was covered in bandages. His hair stood on end like a brush, but he felt much better.

'Look at you, you hero,' said Rusham.

'I'd rather be a hero than an accident-prone old man,' said Clavity. 'What do you think Reynard's up to now? We can't have him running off after Krankhausen on his own, now can we?'

'I think they're preparing for an assault,' said Rusham.

Clavity frowned. It would be typical of Reynard to take all the glory. According to the rumour mill, it was how he had won his promotion in the first place.

'I'm going to check on Sean. Don't go anywhere, Major.'

Clavity rattled his stretcher in protest. It was no use; he was pinned down by a blanket and straps. He felt like a mummy being posted by airmail.

'I don't suppose you could...'

Rusham watched him wriggle around and smiled.

'And spoil your bed rest, Major? Not a chance. You heard the medic.'

Rusham stepped out into the corridor and was almost knocked over.

'Watch out, love! Coming through!'

She sidestepped two burly commandos who were wheeling a long, black missile towards the front of the aircraft. They wore full body armour and what appeared to be glide suits. Across their shoulders they carried weapons she had not seen before. Rusham winced as they bulldozed their way past. She heard another pair of commandos approaching and hurried up the stairs ahead of them.

'Nice of you to keep us informed, Captain,' she muttered.

'This is Reynard; Assault Teams prepare for deployment in ten minutes,' said a speaker on the wall.

Rusham gave a wry smile. Clavity would be annoyed to be missing out on the action.

Skyraptor-one turned to face Krankhausen's base. Determined to watch the assault, Sean undid his seat belt and moved to get a better view. He watched the platform smoulder, but something was different. He studied a screen hanging from the ceiling to find out what it was. They approached the platform like a cat stalking a mouse. Ahead of them, Deuce glinted before its camouflage adjusted and it blended back into its surroundings.

'Enjoying the view?' said Reynard.

'Err, yes,' said Sean, taken aback. 'But what's that hanging from Krankhausen's base?'

Sean pointed at the main screen. Suspended beneath the platform was a torpedo-shaped object, which seemed to be moving towards the sea. Reynard moved a joystick on his command console and zoomed in for a closer look.

'He's trying to escape! Well spotted, Sean.'

'Weapons, I need a precise laser strike,' said Reynard.

'Where, sir?'

'Your target is on the main screen now.'

The image zoomed in to show a small, grey submarine being lowered by four cables. It was elliptical in shape, with fins fore and aft.

'Aim for the winching gear,' said Reynard, highlighting a mechanism on the screen.

'Powering up the laser now.'

'Fire when ready,' said Reynard.

Sean watched the winch glow yellow and white. Sparks burst from within, as the metal deformed and gave way. The submarine juddered and came to a halt.

'Pierce the sub as well,' said Reynard.

There was a sudden flash of red light from the platform, and Skyraptor-two appeared in full view. It was damaged on its near-side, and smoke poured from a burning gash in its hull. Behind its wings, two horizontal fans span in a hazy blur, while at its tail, two engines pounded the waves in wide circles of exhaust fumes.

'Sunbeam, this is Deuce, we are taking incoming fire, over.'

'Do you need to withdraw?' said Reynard.

'Negative, Sunbeam, we have contained the damage and begun to deploy our assault teams. Can you provide covering fire, over?'

'Will do, Deuce. Weapons, locate the incoming laser and destroy it.'

'Yes, sir.'

Two more laser beams struck Krankhausen's base, and the submarine lurched downwards. A coupling at one end gave way, and a cable fell into the sea. Another laser cut into the submarine's hull, which promptly caught fire. Meanwhile, a small dome on the platform exploded.

'We have disabled the hostile's laser, sir,' said Weapons.

'Excellent. Flight, take us in for a closer look,' said Reynard.

Sean watched three flattened missiles emerge from the mouth of Skyraptor-two. As they hovered past, he realised the missiles had double V-shaped wings and figures hunched behind raised fairings. The strange craft threw out jets of flame and accelerated towards Krankhausen's base.

****

Greerbo staggered onto the viewing deck weighed down by a cache of weapons. Over his shoulders, he carried a missile launcher, a machine gun and a portable laser. He dropped the machine gun, which clanked on the metal walkway. Krankhausen strode ahead of him and marched up to the railings. He raised his binoculars and studied the sky using infra-red filters.

'Hurry up, Greerbo, I've spotted them!'

Greerbo dropped the rest of the weapons in a heap on the deck.

'Launch the missile!' said Krankhausen.

Greerbo picked up a long tube and aimed it at an empty sky.

'But what am I firing at, boss?'

'Straight ahead,' said Krankhausen, pointing at a patch of cloud in the distance.

'Where?'

Krankhausen let out a snarl.

'Just fire, will you?'

Greerbo unleashed the missile. It spiralled through the air, unguided, before splashing into the sea, wide of its intended target.

'Useless!' said Krankhausen.

'But, boss…'

'Don't boss me!' snapped Krankhausen.

Tiny aircraft appeared out of nowhere, flying low above the sea. Through his binoculars, Krankhausen spotted a Foundation aircraft. It hovered with its loading ramp extended. He watched commandos emerge and realised they would arrive within minutes. He began to panic.

'Give me the laser!' he said, snatching it from Greerbo. 'And fetch the Matteract! Hurry!'

'Yes, boss,' said Greerbo.

Krankhausen steadied himself against a railing and took aim. He used one hand to hold the laser and his other to focus the binoculars. It was not an easy task. Satisfied with his aim, Krankhausen squeezed the fire button and held it down. The laser unleashed a burst of light and struck home.

'Yes!' he cried.

A small patch on one side of the Foundation aircraft began to smoke. Krankhausen tried to fire again, but the laser beeped and nothing happened.

'Pathetic weapon!' he said and hurled the spent weapon across the deck. Where were his beautiful drones when he needed them?

Greerbo returned carrying a grey, fluted tube attached to a cylinder and a trigger assembly. A series of pipes encircled its barrel, and a trailing lead connected the device to a power pack. Krankhausen licked his lips.

'Help me to set it up, Greerbo,' he said, taking hold of the lighter end of the weapon.

Greerbo grunted and dragged the power pack behind him.

'When is it my turn, boss?'

'When I say so,' said Krankhausen.

By now, the first commandos were in range. Krankhausen ignored them and aimed at the damaged Skyraptor hovering in full view. The Matteract whined for a moment before releasing its deadly rays. A burst of invisible particles sped across the water and boiled a corridor of seawater. It swept past two miniature aircraft and struck the Skyraptor on its wing.

'Gotcha!' said Krankhausen.

Greerbo cheered and shook his fist. The damaged Skyraptor span and ducked wildly in the air. Surely it was only a matter of time until it crashed into the sea? Krankhausen fired again, but the Matteract was dead. At that moment, he realised the battle was over. What few weapons they had left would only delay the inevitable, and now his submarine was crippled.

'It was good though wasn't it?' he said, flushed with triumph at hitting the Skyraptor.

'Yes, boss,' said Greerbo. 'Remember, we still have the drone ships?'

'Then what are we waiting for?' said Krankhausen, grinning.

They turned to leave but could not resist a chuckle at the stricken Skyraptor.

****

'Mayday! Mayday! This is Deuce, we're going down!'

Skyraptor-two wheeled around, and its pilot battled for

control. Sean noticed half a wing had vanished in a burst of heat and steam. Its opposite pair had also been damaged and hung, offering no lift. Behind it, the remains of an engine spewed out smoke and pieces of shrapnel. The Skyraptor veered and dipped towards the sea. It balanced on its two remaining engines and lurched sideways before being corrected by its pilot.

'Abandon ship! Abandon ship! Deploy all commandos and support crew.'

Reynard was in shock. His first instinct was to lash out and destroy Krankhausen's base in revenge. However, he reconsidered. The entire mission depended on his next decision, and he knew it.

'Weapons, fire stun grenades at those two jokers.'

Soon the commandos would reach Krankhausen. Soon their mission would be over. It would be men against boys or in this case highly equipped rhinos against a short, stocky man and a pasty-faced stick insect.

'Grenades away, sir,' said Weapons.

Reynard glanced at the main screen and watched the projectiles flash towards Krankhausen's base. It was like watching in slow-motion, and Reynard soon regretted his decision. The first grenade hit a railing and exploded some distance from the two figures. The second bounced and hit the stocky man full in the chest, knocking him over. It exploded on the deck and sent both men sprawling.

'Was that our suspect, Captain?' said Rusham, returning to the flight deck.

'What's left of him,' said Reynard, embarrassed.

'Any chance of someone picking up the pieces?'

'Our first assault team will be there any second.'

The stocky man lay flat on his back, his head dangling above the sea, but there was no sign of Krankhausen.

'Better start looking in the water then,' said Rusham.

Reynard blanched and tapped his neckpiece to relay the orders.

Sean stepped forwards and pointed at Krankhausen's platform.

'They've arrived,' he said, in a calm voice.

'Who have, Sean? The commandos?' said Rusham.

Sean closed his eyes, and a vision of swirling water filled his mind.

'The others. They're here.'

'Sunbeam, this is Deuce, our engines can't hold much longer. We're preparing to ditch. And we could use anything that floats right now, over.'

'Deuce, we're coming to assist,' said Reynard. 'Briggs, prepare to launch our life rafts.'

Sean's legs gave way. He felt Rusham reach out and catch him before he fell to the floor.

'What's the matter with him?' said Reynard.

'I think he's fainted,' said Rusham.

But Sean was wide awake and stared at a pair of cold, dark eyes.

****

Jenkins crept across the office floor on his hands and knees. He heard footsteps in the corridor and watched shadows pass the office window. From their shapes and sounds, he realised they were commandos. They were most likely heading towards the armoury lift.

'You won't find me out there,' he whispered.

Jenkins tried the door handle. It was locked. He tiptoed to the office desk and rifled through the top drawer. Sure enough, on a plastic tray, he found a spare door key and a lighter.

'Tut-tut,' he said and took both.

Jenkins returned to the door and tested the key. He felt its lock mechanism clunk and turn. Satisfied there was no one approaching, he dropped to his hands and knees and opened the door a couple of inches. The corridor looked much as he remembered and, more importantly, it was deserted. However, a sudden noise on his left made him jump. There were footsteps, and a communicator crackled into life. A commando reported in. Fortunately, he had not spotted a face peering around a door frame at shin height.

Jenkins crept back into the office and pulled the door to. He waited for the commando's footsteps to fade and sprang into action. First, he wheeled a pedestal out from under the desk and used it as a doorstop. Next, he dragged the coat stand across the room and mounted it on top of the pedestal. And finally, he prised a small whiteboard from a wall and propped it up behind the base of the coat stand. He pushed his shaky contraption out into the corridor and veered left, zigzagging as he went.

Without warning, two commandos appeared from around the corner. Jenkins realised his plan would fail. They paused for a second, bemused by the sight in front of them, and Jenkins charged. He was quick, but not quick enough. The first commando raised his rifle and fired a neat pattern of holes through the whiteboard. The bullets missed Jenkins' head by a whisker.

'Play nicely!' he cried and rammed the coat stand into the first commando's groin.

The commando howled and grabbed his colleague, pulling him off-balance. This gave Jenkins a few valuable seconds. He turned and sprinted back down the corridor. Gunfire sounded, and a bullet clipped the top of his shoulder. But Jenkins was gone. He dived headfirst into a waste disposal chute and slid all the way to the basement. He felt a rush of adrenalin and a harsh sting from his wound.

'Soon it will be your turn to feel pain,' he growled.

CHAPTER 13: OLD SCHOOL

Lieutenant Marsh paced the length of Skyraptor-two and checked his crew had evacuated. He secured the bulkhead doors and activated the Skyraptor's floatation devices. Compressors roared and filled the inside of the aircraft with inflated helium cushions. Marsh realised he was fortunate to have this opportunity. If Krankhausen had been a better shot, they would have been at the bottom of the ocean by now. Or worse, they would be vapour. Marsh reached the flight deck and found the pilot and co-pilot struggling with the controls.

'We can't hold her much longer, sir,' said the pilot.

'Okay, let's do it. Ditch all our weapons,' said Marsh.

'Weapons released, sir,' said the co-pilot, in a deadpan voice.

Beneath them, missiles, torpedoes, and mines plunged into the sea, but not a single one exploded.

'Weapons bay empty and sealed, sir.'

'Good, when you're ready, gentlemen.'

The pilot and co-pilot read through an onscreen checklist.

'We need breathing masks, sir,' said the pilot.

'I'll fetch them,' said Marsh.

He raised a floor panel marked in red and hauled out two bags of emergency equipment. Among other things, they contained survival kits, lifejackets, an inflatable boat and portable breathing masks.

'Shame you don't have a spare wing in there,' said the pilot.

In theory, Skyraptors were designed to float for several hours but that was with a full set of wings. To make matters worse, the pilots had to seal up the rear engine, which meant landing in the sea using only one hover motor.

'Here,' said Marsh, brandishing a pair of masks.

He helped the pilot and co-pilot to pull them over their

faces and strapped himself into a seat.

'Make it a good one, Flight.'

'Will do, sir,' said the pilot.

Marsh attached his own mask, and the pilot began the countdown.

'Three, two, one, now.'

The rear engine stopped, and the aircraft lurched downwards. By keeping the remaining engine on full throttle, they slowed a little, before veering sharply to the right and plunging into the sea.

On impact, the three men were thrown forwards. Marsh watched seawater dim the cockpit until the interior lights came on. It was an eerie sight.

'If we had to eject now would it work?'

'I've no idea, sir, it's never been tested underwater to my knowledge,' said the pilot.

'We'd have to use the escape hatch and free dive to the surface,' said the co-pilot.

The Skyraptor sank for a few moments, before slowly rising. It stayed low in the water and tipped sideways towards its intact wings.

Reynard watched with a heavy heart.

'Captain, two surface vessels are approaching from the west,' said Radar.

'Show me their positions.'

'On screen now, sir. They'll be in range within ten minutes.'

It was too soon for rescue craft, and in any case, the recovery teams would arrive from the north.

'Perhaps no one's told Krankhausen he's lost yet?' said Rusham.

'Either way, we have to protect Deuce and her crew,' said Reynard.

'Flight, let's take a closer look.'

'Yes, sir.'

Sean woke from his trance and looked around the flight

deck. Rusham was sitting beside him.

'How are you feeling?' said Rusham.

'We need to save the commandos.'

'Save them from who?'

'From them,' said Sean, pointing at the smoking platform.

'Our commandos are as tough as nails, Sean. They can look after themselves,' said Rusham.

Two commandos, Chan and Stevens, flew on a level course towards Krankhausen's base. They had rehearsed their attack plan at least a dozen times in virtual reality, but this time it was for real. Behind them, two more assault teams followed on either side. Chan needed to get it right, and he knew it. His first goal was to find a safe landing site. Given the state of the charred platform, it would not be easy.

'I'm going to fly past and take a closer look.'

'Copy that,' said Stevens.

Their TAC, or Two-person Attack Craft, raced over the sea at over eighty knots. It was lightweight and agile, but it had a limited range. To be effective, Chan and Stevens had to work as one, which took months of training.

'How's our fuel burn?' said Chan.

'Fine, provided we land soon,' said Stevens.

'Okay, I'm going to buzz the main dome. Get ready to return fire,' said Chan.

'Locked and loaded,' said Stevens, priming his weapon.

Chan slowed to seventy knots and steered the TAC into a shallow climb. Behind him, Stevens steadied his weapon.

'We'll be there in thirty seconds,' said Chan.

Ahead of them, the sea began to bubble furiously, and a ring of foam became visible around Krankhausen's base. Chan thought nothing of it and continued his approach.

'What's happening down there?' said Stevens, preparing his trigger finger.

A huge waterspout rose from the sea. At an alarming pace, it spiralled upwards and widened, becoming a wall of seething water in front of Krankhausen's base.

'Hold on!' cried Chan, accelerating into a steep turn

The thundering water stretched outwards until it surrounded the entire platform. There was nothing Chan could do. Their TAC hit the waterspout head on and was carried upwards, end over end. The vortex snapped their safety tethers and threw the commandos into the sea like rag dolls.

****

In the basement at Foundation HQ, Jenkins rubbed his sore limbs. He had landed in a heap on a bare concrete floor and ached all over. His shoulder ached, and his knees began to bleed.

'Typical!' he said, cursing the lack of rubbish to cushion his fall.

Jenkins sat in a large, airless space. It contained a compactor and furnace on one side, and a heating system on the other. Apart from the constant hum of an air conditioning unit, everything was quiet. He considered a row of metal cupboards. From memory, he knew they housed circuit breakers and meters, but he was looking for something far more interesting. Jenkins turned his attention to the heating system.

His mind raced with scenes of a house under attack. Foundation commandos unleashed a barrage of gunfire. Windows shattered and brickwork was damaged in the onslaught. His sister cowered beside a bedroom cupboard, while bullet holes peppered the walls around her. One of the commandos fired a smoke grenade, which crashed through a bedroom window and set light to the curtains. As the flames began to spread, Jenkins felt a rage grow inside him. How could Cuthbertson forgive himself after what he'd done? The Foundation was supposed to protect the innocent.

He limped to the heating system and looked for its control box. He found it mounted on a wall, several feet from the burner. It had a metal cover secured by a twisted wire and plastic tag. Jenkins sighed in disgust and stretched the seal apart using his screwdriver. On his second attempt, it gave way, and he tore the cover open. Jenkins switched off the gas burner and was greeted by stillness. Now the fun could begin. He set to work wrenching pipes from the unit and opening valves. The unmistakable smell of gas wafted under his nose, and Jenkins hurried away in search of an exit.

****

Skyraptor-one flew high above the sea and scanned the horizon. Two hydrofoils appeared on the main screen. They were heading towards them at a tremendous speed.

'Radar, do you have a lock?' said Reynard.

'No, sir, I can't get a fix. It's like they're jamming our signals.'

'Not again?' said Reynard. 'How are they doing this?'

'They must know our technology, sir,' said Radar.

Reynard sighed.

'Is there any chance they're friendly?'

'I've tried signalling them on all international frequencies, sir,' said Comms. 'They're not replying.'

Sean was overcome with frustration. He rose from his seat and confronted Reynard.

'Can't you see?' They're here. *They're* doing this!'

'Enough!' said Reynard. 'We have serious work to do. Agent Rusham?'

Rusham stepped forwards and reached for Sean's arm.

'Don't touch me!' said Sean, breaking free.

'It's okay,' said Rusham. 'We'll look after you.'

Sean allowed himself to be led back to his seat.

'Why doesn't anyone ever listen to me?' he said.

Rusham gave a half smile.

'I'm listening, Sean. What can you tell me?'

'It's all a blur,' said Sean. 'But I know something evil is out there watching us.'

Reynard rolled his eyes and turned back to the main

screen.

'We need to disable those hydrofoils and quickly. Does anyone have any ideas?'

'We could guide our missiles by sight,' said Weapons.

'Yeah, one at a time,' said Flight.

'And what if they're shot down?' said Reynard. 'The hydrofoils are bound to have defences.'

On screen, the hydrofoils sped towards them in a battle formation. Reynard zoomed in on their angular shapes, which were still on the horizon.

'Or we could EMP the whole area,' said Weapons.

'With a Skyraptor and commandos in the water?' said Reynard. 'Come on guys; we must have some better options?'

The flight deck fell silent for a moment.

'Why don't you try what they did in the Second World War?' said Sean.

'Meaning?' said Reynard.

'Submarines used to launch a fan of torpedoes at a convoy.'

Reynard looked dubious.

'It would at least force them to change course, sir,' said Weapons.

'It might slow them down, but how do we stop them?' said Reynard.

'We could launch our own TACs?' said Flight. 'They should at least be able to damage them?'

'Good thinking!' said Reynard.

'Weapons, prepare to target the nearest hydrofoil with a spread of three torpedoes.'

'Right away, sir.'

Reynard switched on the ship's intercom.

'Sergeant Briggs, prepare to deploy Assault Teams One, Two and Three.'

'Briggs here, sir, what are their orders?'

'Two hydrofoils are approaching from the west. We need them disabled. Repeat, disable the hydrofoils.'

There was a crackle and a muffled sound of orders being

relayed.

'Confirmed, Captain, the Assault Teams will scramble and engage.'

'Good luck, men, we're counting on you,' said Reynard.

'Torpedoes away, sir,' said Weapons.

'What do we have left?' said Reynard.

'One torpedo and six missiles.'

Reynard considered the situation. They had enough munitions to ward off the hydrofoils but not enough to guarantee a victory.

'Flight, hold us steady, we need to protect our men in the water. Weapons, prepare the lasers and cannon.'

'Will do, sir.'

'Captain, you need to hear this,' said Comms.

'Patch them through,' said Reynard.

'Sunbeam, this is Deuce, over.'

'Go ahead, Deuce.'

'We've ditched, but we're still floating.'

'Good work, Lieutenant. The recovery teams will be here soon.'

'The trouble is we're being pulled towards a huge wave.'

'Say again?' said Reynard, not believing his ears.

'On screen now, sir,' said Radar.

'Mon Dieu!' said Reynard. 'What in the world is that?'

The main screen showed an enormous wall of swirling water surrounding Krankhausen's base. The platform itself was almost hidden.

****

Content with his work, Jenkins staggered to the lift shaft. He found a small maintenance hatch and turned two levers to release its cover. The levers creaked but did not release the hatch.

'Come on!' he cried.

Enraged, Jenkins sat down and pounded the hatch using the soles of his feet. The punishment was relentless, and his feet began to bleed. After numerous impacts, the concrete casing cracked, and the hatch fell inwards.

'Hey! Who's there?' said a voice from above.

'Your worst nightmare,' whispered Jenkins, crawling into the lift shaft.

He balanced on a ledge and felt his way in the dark, while laser-sights flickered back and forth searching for a target. Jenkins felt along the wall and found a piece of cold metal jutting out from the concrete. It was the escape ladder. He grinned and reached into the waistband of his shorts. The lighter was still there. From the open hatch came a pungent smell of gas. Jenkins began to climb.

'Halt!' cried a voice.

Two shots ricocheted off the walls, and Jenkins laughed to himself.

'Is that the best you can do?'

As he climbed, he realised he was in the wrong lift shaft. The armoury was deep underground, but the ladder only led upwards.

'There's more than one way to punish a traitor,' whispered Jenkins.

CHAPTER 14: DRASTIC ACTION

Sean followed Agent Rusham to the medical bay. He was still annoyed with Reynard for ignoring his warnings, but at least his torpedo idea had been put into practice.

'Let's see how grumpy-drawers is doing,' said Rusham.

Clavity grunted and opened his eyes. He was lying on a narrow stretcher-bed attached to the wall.

'Hi, Major,' said Sean, in a deflated voice.

'What's wrong? I thought we were winning?'

'It's getting weird out there,' said Rusham.

'And *they've* arrived,' said Sean.

'Who's arrived? The recovery teams?'

Sean noticed Clavity struggle to free himself and knelt to loosen straps on his bed. Clavity sat up, despite Rusham's disapproving look.

'I don't know,' said Sean. 'But I can feel something evil out there and it's taken Krankhausen.'

'*What?*' said Clavity.

'No one can see anything because of that waterspout,' said Rusham. 'And the hydrofoils don't help.'

'What waterspout? What hydrofoils?' said Clavity. 'And what is Reynard doing about this?'

'Panicking mostly,' said Rusham.

Clavity flushed.

'And you think someone's turned up to rescue Krankhausen?'

'Err, *yeah*,' said Sean.

Clavity gave Rusham a look of thunder.

'But there's no way through it, Major. The waterspout's surrounded Krankhausen's base.'

'Can't we go over it or under it?' said Clavity.

'Have you seen how powerful it is?' said Rusham.

Sean laughed at the squabbling agents.

'And I suppose *you* have a better idea?' said Clavity.

Sean was taken aback for a moment. He spread his hands wide and gave a weak grin.

'We could make a hole in it?'

'Are you joking?' said Rusham. 'It's enormous! And it's already wiped out our best commandos.'

'Hold that thought,' said Clavity, raising a hand to calm things. 'What if we *could* punch a hole in this waterspout?'

'Just like Krankhausen did when he broke into my bedroom,' said Sean, his eyes ablaze.

Clavity smiled.

'You're a genius!'

'I don't understand,' said Rusham.

'How many TACs do we have on board?'

Rusham pursed her lips.

'About five, I guess.'

'And what's mounted on a TAC?' said Clavity.

'Whatever you like. A machine gun, a laser or a grenade launcher.'

'What about a Matteract?'

'You're not serious?' said Rusham, pulling a face.

Clavity nodded.

'But who's going to fly it?' said Rusham, staring at Clavity's bandages.

'Do you think Reynard's going to lend us any of his commandos?' said Clavity.

Rusham shook her head.

'Which means Krankhausen will get away.'

Rusham let out a sigh.

'Alright, I'll do it. But I'll need someone to fire the Matteract.'

'I'll go!' said Sean.

Rusham and Clavity eyed each other.

'We can't, can we?'

'Who else can we trust?' said Clavity.

****

Agent Lee felt her watch buzz and read an incoming message.

'The Foundation is on Red Alert. All agents must report to HQ immediately. Report to Security on arrival.'

'Hmm, looks like the party's over.'

She considered how best to manage the situation. Her team would need to pack the van and bring Mrs Yeager along with them. Which would be fun. She was still climbing the walls after her son's disappearance. Well, what was left of her walls. Lee had tried to reassure her that Sean was in safe hands. However, Mrs Yeager had launched into a full-blown rant for at least twenty minutes. Lee went in search of her second-in-command.

'We could always tell her we're going to collect her son?' said Brown.

'Sure, and you can explain why he's not at HQ when we get there.'

Brown gave a pained expression.

'Right, let's load up and ship out,' said Lee.

****

Professor Quark followed Ayres down a fire escape staircase. Ahead of them, three commandos scanned the stairwell using laser-sights.

'How long has Jenkins been in there?' said Quark.

'I don't know, Professor. Ten, maybe twenty minutes?'

'I heard he floored one of your men?'

'It was more like three,' said Ayres. 'He's a wild animal.'

'But he's only tiny,' said Quark.

'It took four men just to restrain him.'

'And yet he escaped?'

'Indeed,' said Ayres. 'I've never seen anything like it.'

At the bottom of the staircase, they reached a fire door. It was locked. The commandos looked to their leader for guidance.

'Best stand bank, Professor,' said Ayres, skipping down the last few steps. 'Alright lads, we'll have to blow it off its hinges.'

****

Rusham led Sean to the forward loading ramp. The cargo bay was empty except for two TACs sat on their cradles. One was flight-ready and was parked facing the open ramp. Rusham tried to remember the last time she had flown one. It must have been years ago. A strong breeze ruffled her hair.

'Can I help you?' said a voice.

Rusham froze and squinted in the daylight. A man dressed in camouflage stood beside the ramp controls. He was as wide as he was tall, and Rusham realised he was a Sergeant.

'Well?' said Briggs.

'Captain Reynard wants to see you on the flight deck,' said Rusham, putting on her brightest smile.

Briggs considered this and rubbed his neck.

'Then why didn't he call me on the intercom?'

'Apparently, it's playing up,' said Rusham, trying to sound convincing.

Briggs glared at her.

'Right then, jump to it!' he said, marching towards the rear of the cargo bay. 'We can't keep the Captain waiting now, can we?'

Rusham winked at Sean.

'Captain Reynard told us to wait in the medical bay.'

'Quite right too,' said Briggs. 'Carry on.'

Briggs reached the metal staircase and began to climb to the flight deck. As he did so, Rusham pulled Sean to one side.

'Let's go,' she whispered, hurrying back to the ramp.

Rusham untied the TAC's restraints as quickly as she could and searched a locker for flight gear.

'Here, put these on,' she said, thrusting a helmet, jacket and life vest into Sean's arms.

Sean put on the jacket and tightened the life vest. It was

far too big and smothered his narrow frame. The helmet was a better fit, and he fastened it under his chin.

'And clip yourself on here,' said Rusham, pointing at a metal D-ring on the TAC.

'Huh?' said Sean.

Rusham clipped and unclipped the tether on her life vest to demonstrate.

'Right, got it,' said Sean, clambering onto his seat.

'And hold on tight. You'll find handles and footrests on either side.'

Sean felt a tingling in his stomach. He attached his tether and rested his sneakers on the footrests. It was a streamlined machine, and the prospect of flying it made him shudder with excitement. Meanwhile, Rusham returned carrying a weapon and clamped it onto the TAC in front of him. She adjusted its barrel and slid it sideways, before tightening some levers at its base. She climbed onto the pilot's seat and put on her own helmet.

'See if you can touch the trigger, but don't pull it,' she said over the intercom.

Sean discovered he could only reach the trigger if he released his tether. A tiny detail he decided to keep to himself.

'Yes, I can,' he said, re-attaching himself.

Rusham switched on the TAC and flicked through its controls in a hurry.

'Whatever you do, don't fire until I tell you. Seriously, Sean, that Matteract could melt a whole ship in seconds and we'll only have one chance.'

'Got it,' said Sean.

He peered over Rusham's shoulder at the expanse of ocean and began to have second thoughts. What if they crashed or were shot down?

'Hey! What are you doing?' cried a voice behind them.

It was Briggs.

'Get off there this instant! That's commando property!'

'Hold on!' said Rusham.

Sean's heart skipped a beat and his adrenalin kicked-in. Briggs ran towards them waving his fist, and Rusham lit up the TAC's engines. She gunned its throttle and sent them hurtling out of the cargo bay. Sean gripped the TAC for all he was worth and was still flung backwards. He managed to stay onboard thanks to his safety harness and their sudden plunge towards the sea.

Reynard waited for news from his assault teams. He watched the hydrofoils close in and avoid the torpedoes with ease. On his nearest monitor, he identified several missile canisters on their decks.

'Our sensors are still out of action, sir,' said Radar.

'Flight, prepare to withdraw,' said Reynard.

From beneath them came the sudden roar of a jet engine.

'What was that?' said the pilot, straining to peer over his controls.

'Rusham!' said Reynard, in a fury.

'Our loading bay door is jammed open, sir. It's not responding,' said Weapons.

'And our flight controls, sir. We're stuck in hover-mode.'

Reynard tried to take it all in. Jammed controls, approaching missile ships and a disobedient agent were all he needed. His eyelid started to twitch.

'Look!' said Weapons, pointing at the main screen.

The nearest hydrofoil had slowed to a halt and began to rotate a missile launcher towards them. They watched in horror as it tilted upwards.

'Do we have any weapons operational?' said Reynard.

'Only short-range cannon, sir.'

'Weapons, come with me,' said Reynard, leaping out of his chair. 'I have a plan!'

CHAPTER 15: SPARKS

Professor Quark received urgent news from his team. He tried to phone Cuthbertson, but his calls went straight to voicemail. In frustration, he left a message.

'What's the point of a mobile phone if no one answers it?' he grumbled to himself.

His team had at last restored the main computer system. The original computers were only fit for the scrap heap. Krankhausen's viruses had ravaged their programs and hard drives in seconds, leaving only burnt out circuit boards. However, despite the budget cuts, Quark's team had tucked away some old computers. He considered presenting Cuthbertson with a large bill for repairs when the emergency was over.

Quark had asked his team to review Jenkins' files in more detail. They discovered someone had gone to great lengths to forge Jenkins' records going back many years. The changes were so well executed, it was now difficult to tell the truth from fiction. He also asked his team to check Jenkins' details against secret government and police records. As expected, they pieced together a consistent picture about Jenkins and his parents. However, there was not a single mention of his sister. Nor was there a birth certificate, a school registration or medical records. It was as if Jenkins' sister had never existed.

Quark's nose twitched, and he turned his attention to the basement. A familiar smell like rotten eggs had irritated his nose.

'Stop! I can smell gas!' he cried.

Ayres waved his men away from the fire door. They reluctantly lowered their weapons.

'I can't smell anything, Professor,' said Ayres, inside his combat helmet and facemask.

The commandos looked to Quark for an explanation.
'Stand back,' he said, pulling a device from his jacket pocket.

It was black with a silver cone and a small screen. Quark swept it around the stairwell and approached the fire door. The commandos shuffled out of his way huffing and puffing. Although the fire door was tightly sealed, Quark's sensor beeped. An orange symbol flashed on its screen and turned red as he approached the door.

'Methane,' said Quark. 'It seems our friend Jenkins has been meddling with the gas supply.'

'I knew he was up to something,' said Ayres. 'What should we do?'

Quark paused for thought.

'First, we need to cut off the gas supply. Then we need to pump the basement full of flame retardant.'

'Come on, team, you heard the Professor,' said Ayres, leading his men upstairs.

****

Jenkins continued his climb in total darkness. It was hard work, and although his body was pumped full of adrenalin he began to tire. Laser-sights scanned the lift shaft, but the voices were now below him and distant. He chuckled to himself. It had been so easy to slip past the guards. The fools had assumed they could use the lift car to block his path. Little did they realise, he had squeezed past in the crevice where the ladder was mounted. He paused for a moment and felt vibrations in the ladder. Someone was following him.

Jenkins bumped his head against something hard and unyielding. He reared back in surprise and almost fell. It was a concrete ceiling. On a lower rung, he fumbled in his waistband. The lighter was still there, and he sparked it into life. Its tiny flame revealed a shaft wall caked in dirt and oil. Above him, was a concrete shelf and winching gear. However, there was no sign of a maintenance hatch. Jenkins rubbed and scraped at the wall using his bare hands.

'Hold it right there!' said a voice below.

Jenkins realised he was running out of time. He stepped down a few rungs and continued to scrape at the wall. His fingernail caught something metallic. Could it be a hinge? Or a catch? His nail broke, but he ignored the pain and rubbed away more layers of grime. He felt a metal seal in the wall and traced it with his fingers. Meanwhile, his left hand began to sting from the heat of the lighter. He ignored the pain and continued to search for an escape hatch.

'Crack!'

A shot grazed Jenkins on his left wrist. He recoiled instinctively and let go of the lighter. It vanished into the gloom, and he braced himself. He heard it strike the shaft wall and clatter against the lift car. But there was no explosion. Jenkins cursed his bad luck and felt a wet trickle of blood ooze from his wrist. He felt relieved they were only using bullets, a blaster bolt would have seared his wrist in two.

'Ping!'

Another shot passed by and ricocheted. This time it whistled close to his head. Jenkins found a metal handle and turned it anti-clockwise. Surprisingly, it moved, as if lubricated by the grime. He gave it a hard shove and a hatch door fell outwards. It struck a commando full on his helmet, and Jenkins crawled out through the opening. He landed head first on top of an unconscious commando and helped himself to his blaster and sidearm.

'Just what I was looking for,' he said, with a grin.

****

Greaves was determined to make up for his earlier mistakes. Two of his best guards were in the medical wing, and he was convinced people were mocking him after Jenkins' escape. He helped himself to a blaster, torch and body armour and was ready for action. Jenkins had long since escaped to the basement, and Greaves tracked his progress by listening to reports on his neckpiece. He knew Ayres had sealed off the area and instructed everyone to await orders, but Greaves had other ideas.

'I'll get you, sonny boy,' he said, switching his blaster to full power. 'No one makes a fool out of me.'

Greaves jogged up a flight of stairs and followed in Jenkins' footsteps. He found the first-floor corridor empty except for a plastic seal over a hole in the wall. All traces of furniture had been cleared away, and there were only a few scrape marks on the floor.

'A waste chute, how appropriate for trash like you,' said Greaves.

He cut the seal using a knife and stood back. There was a rush of air as the pressure equalised. If his sense of smell had been keener, Greaves would have stopped right there. Unfortunately, after a climbing accident, Greaves could not even smell a clove of garlic pressed against his nose. Which may also have explained the body odour problems he was reminded of on a daily basis. Greaves climbed into the waste chute feet first and sat on its outer edge. He steadied himself and took a deep breath, ready to confront Jenkins.

'Hey, you! Stop right there!' said a voice behind him.

A commando sprinted down the corridor. Greaves let go and tried to slide away, but his body armour snagged against the metal rim. He wriggled his hips to break free but found his wrists clamped in the commando's vice-like grip.

'Get your mutton hands off me!'

'Don't you get it? The basement's full of gas!' said the commando. 'One spark and the whole place will go up!'

Greaves realised his mistake and tried to clamber out of the chute. However, as he tensed his thighs, he struck a webbing clip holding his torch. The clip pinged open, and the torch rolled along the edge of the chute before sliding downwards. Greaves swung his legs to try and catch it, but the torch slipped past and was gone.

****

Lee and her team drove back to headquarters through heavy traffic. Throughout the journey, Mrs Yeager had been giving the agents a tongue-lashing. They had apparently destroyed her garden, killed her cat, poisoned her, kidnapped her son and made her chimney and roof collapse. Her lawyers would be contacted and everyone was certain to lose their jobs. All in all, it was turning out to be a most entertaining trip.

Mrs Yeager also threatened to jump from the van, unless her son was returned immediately. While Lee was tempted to let her try, she realised she would be held responsible and locked the van's doors centrally. The medic had also refused to give Mrs Yeager any more treatment in case it caused a heart attack. He failed to specify who was most at risk of the heart attack – Agent Lee, the medic or Mrs Yeager? Mercifully, the van was equipped with noise cancelling headphones, and Lee put some on. She relaxed in her seat surrounded by blissful tones of music.

A while later, they reached an area of parkland and approached a large, white building set back from the road. At first sight, it looked similar to a business park.

'Welcome to Foundation Headquarters,' said Lee.

Mrs Yeager was sure to be making caustic remarks, and Lee chuckled to herself that she could not hear a single word. The van pulled into a driveway and approached a gatehouse. Lee showed her pass, and they were waved through. As they drove on, an optical illusion was revealed. The white building was surrounded by an immense wall and a sunken moat, hidden from the main road. The van followed a steep slope and entered a tunnel, where it was sprayed with decontaminant gas. Lasers searched the van for threats, while a row of metal bins flashed in unison as they passed by. To Lee's relief, they were recognised, and the sentries did not open fire.

'Here we go,' said Lee, as they emerged into daylight.

The driver pulled up under a covered area, and Lee unlocked the van.

'Everybody out! Agent Brown, please escort Mrs Yeager. All other agents report to Security.'

The reception area was vast and swarmed with armed guards. Two huge, rectangular windows dominated the façade, and daylight streamed in through a glass roof. A tiny rainforest stood at the centre of the foyer and had an artificial waterfall, which spread a feeling of calm among most of the new arrivals.

'You'll be safe here, Mrs Yeager,' said Lee, taking off her headphones.

'I was supposed to be safe at home. I want to see Cuthbertson immediately! Do you hear?'

The agents on guard watched the new arrivals and smirked.

'I think the whole country heard you,' said Lee.

'But first, I need a restroom,' said Mrs Yeager.

Lee looked around for someone in charge. What was going on? And why had everyone been summoned to HQ? Mrs Yeager followed Agent Brown across a marble floor to the Visitor's Suite. She refused offers of drinks and instead used her right index finger to full effect, jabbing at anyone who dared to approach.

'It's okay, madam, this building's impregnable,' said a smiling receptionist.

'Boom!'

An almighty explosion shook the floor like an earthquake and threw everyone off their feet. Windows in the foyer cracked and splintered into jagged shards, held together only by micro-engineering and air pressure.

****

Five floors above, Jenkins felt the building shake and grinned.

'Idiots,' he muttered.

He prepared his weapons for action and ran towards Cuthbertson's office. Jenkins' damaged body had blocked all sensations of pain. His gunshot wounds had healed, and his bruises had vanished. Even his cuts were knitting themselves back together. Jenkins had never felt more alive. He sprinted down a carpeted corridor consumed by thoughts of revenge and minutes from his goal.

****

On the first floor, Greaves hurtled out of the waste chute like a cannonball. He flew headfirst towards the opposite wall, dragging his commando helper with him. He came to rest with his boots smoking and scorch marks on his trousers and body armour. The commando groaned beneath him and struggled to roll him away.

'Boy are you in trouble,' said the commando, shifting Greaves into the recovery position.

****

Brigadier Cuthbertson found a quiet corner of the Control Centre and checked his phone messages. Quark had left several, each sounding more urgent than the last. Apparently, the main computer system was now fully operational including the satellite links. Quark also had something important he wanted to share face to face. Cuthbertson sent him a reply by text.

'My office in five minutes.'

Cuthbertson excused himself from the Control Centre and hurried to his private suite. It held one of only a handful of secure connections in the whole building. With any luck, he would be able to access the satellite network and find out if Krankhausen had been caught. They had exchanged a few text messages, but Reynard seemed rather vague, which was unlike him.

The lifts were out of action and Cuthbertson was unused

to climbing. Halfway up the stairs, he paused to catch his breath. He resolved to move his office to the first floor. He was getting too old for all this exertion.

'Damn you, Krankhausen!'

He would be having words with Captain Ayres as well. They should have caught Jenkins ages ago. How hard could it be to capture one man? Cuthbertson reached the third floor pursued by a junior agent.

'Mrs Yeager wants to see you, sir. She says it's urgent.'

'Stuff and nonsense,' said Cuthbertson. 'The woman can wait.'

No sooner had the words left his lips than a huge explosion threw him off balance. He cushioned his fall on his right arm and lay dazed for a moment.

'What in blazes was that?' he cried.

But the junior agent did not hear a word. He was out cold.

'Never mind, I'll find out myself,' said Cuthbertson, staggering up the remaining stairs.

****

Jenkins reached Cuthbertson's office and melted the lock with his blaster. The charred remains of the door swung inwards.

'See? What did I tell you? Call this secure?' he said.

He remembered advising Cuthbertson to make changes to security at HQ. But would he listen? Not a chance. Cuthbertson was too busy going to expensive dinners and the opera. Why the Foundation ever hired Jenkins in the first place was beyond him. It was clear they had no intention of improving their security. And now they would reap what they had sowed.

Jenkins crept inside the room, half expecting to find Cuthbertson waiting for him. The office was luxurious and full of antique furniture. It had lamps, chairs, tables, and a drinks cabinet. It looked more like a gentleman's club than an office. Jenkins sat on a leather chair and began to type at

Cuthbertson's personal computer. Guessing Cuthbertson's password would be the most difficult part of his plan. He remembered some files he had broken into and typed the first thing that came into his head.

'Bounder.'

It was the name of Cuthbertson's favourite dog, an ageing Golden Retriever. Incredibly, Cuthbertson had not changed his password in months, and the computer allowed him access.

'Stupid man,' said Jenkins. 'You're going to pay for your mistakes.'

He clicked on the 'HQ Building' menu and selected 'Site Cleanse'.

'It's time we cleared out the dead wood,' he said to himself. 'And I bet you haven't changed the auto-destruct key?'

Flames filled his mind again. Clara would soon have her revenge. But it would not be served cold. No, his sister would be avenged in a white-hot crater of fusing matter. It was no less than the Foundation deserved.

'Say goodbye, Brigadier,' said Jenkins, as he typed.

CHAPTER 16: TARGET PRACTICE

Reynard stood on the cargo ramp and glared at the trail left by Agent Rusham's TAC. He was joined by the weapons operator and Sergeant Briggs. Skyraptor-one hovered in level flight, a hundred feet above the glistening water. Reynard scanned the deck for weapons. It was empty apart from a spare TAC.

'Sergeant Briggs, we're going to need your help.'

Briggs jumped to attention.

'Help us to move this TAC to the launch position will you?'

'Right away, sir!'

The three men dragged the heavy TAC on its cradle and hauled it out into the daylight. The ramp creaked and groaned under their combined weight.

'Do you think it'll hold, sir?' said Weapons.

'If it can hold a tank it should be able to hold us,' said Reynard.

'Quite right, sir,' said Briggs. 'What are you hoping to do?'

'Whatever we can,' said Reynard.

'Look!' said Weapons. In the distance, the nearest of the hydrofoils had turned towards them. A cloud of white smoke covered its deck and was pierced by a blaze of flames.

'Missile incoming!' said Reynard, into his neckpiece.

'Flight, do you have control?'

'No sir, our controls are still locked.'

'Radar? Any signals?'

'Our tracking system is still down, sir.'

'Listen up, crew, we have incoming missiles. Abandon ship! Repeat, abandon ship!' said Reynard.

The missile stayed low in the sky and raced towards them. Reynard realised they had seconds before impact. He turned his attention to the weapon mounted on the TAC. It was a

Matteract, a crude but effective weapon. He sat behind it, aimed at the incoming missile and fired, but nothing happened. He checked the safety catch and thumped the weapon. Briggs stepped in. He flicked a few switches and gave a thumbs-up.

'Try again, sir. It should be charged any time now.'

The missile swooped in mid-air and thundered ever closer. It was now difficult to spot against the shining sea.

'Where's it gone?' said Reynard.

'One o'clock, sir,' said Weapons.

'I have it.'

Reynard pulled the trigger and prayed. The Matteract hummed and unleashed an invisible beam that vaporised everything in its path.

'Baamm!'

The missile disintegrated, forcing the three men to shield their eyes. Reynard turned back and watched tiny fragments glow and dissolve into thin air. It happened so fast the missile had no time to detonate.

'Missile, incoming!' said Weapons.

The nearest hydrofoil had fired again and was now joined by its sister ship. Reynard aimed the Matteract, but this time the missile had climbed high above them and was difficult to track.

'Sergeant, where are your men?' said Reynard. 'We need those ships destroyed!'

'I'll hurry them up, sir,' said Briggs, clicking on his short-wave radio.

Briggs contacted every assault team in turn. One had run out of fuel and ditched, while the other two were circling in range of the hydrofoils. Briggs ordered them to open fire.

The second missile gained height and began a curved descent. From his vantage point, Reynard could only see its exhaust trail. If he fired, he risked hitting the nose cone of his own aircraft.

'Help me undo this thing!' said Reynard, struggling with the weapon's mounting.

'Allow me, sir,' said Briggs, unscrewing two swivel clips.
But they were too late, the missile had disappeared from view.

'Boom!'

Wreckage from the missile fell from the sky and splashed into the sea.

'What happened?' said Reynard, wiping his brow.

'Our boys happened! Look, half that ship's gone!' said Briggs, pointing at a smoking wreck where the first hydrofoil had been.

'I'll finish them off!' said Reynard, aiming at the smoke.

'They're too far away, sir. All you'll do is boil the sea,' said Weapons.

But Reynard ignored him. Sure enough, a cone of steam stretched across the ocean and stopped short of the wreck. Reynard cursed.

'They've launched another missile, sir!' said Weapons.

A curved trail of smoke approached from the second hydrofoil. Reynard aimed and fired again. This time the Matteract was silent.

'What's the matter with this thing?'

'You've drained its fuel cell,' said Briggs.

'What else do we have?' said Reynard.

Briggs opened a weapons case on the wall.

'Here catch!' he said, throwing blasters to Reynard and Weapons.

The three men took aim and fired repeatedly. However, the missile continued to race towards them unscathed.

'Stand aside, flyboys!' said a voice behind them.

It was Clavity. He staggered forwards carrying a long, rectangular tube on his shoulder and fired. A burst of flames leapt through the cargo deck and narrowly cleared the ceiling.

'What the heck?' cried Reynard, diving for cover.

Clavity stood proudly holding a smoking tube.

'Heat-seeker. Watch her go, boys.'

Sure enough, the heat-seeking missile raced high into the sky and sought out the hostile. The two missiles exploded in a blinding flash above them.

'You could have taken our heads off, Major!' said Reynard.

'Better a few hairs on your head than this whole ship,' said Clavity, smiling. 'Besides, I outrank you, remember?'

Reynard gave a deep scowl.

'Not on this aircraft you don't!'

Briggs received a message on his radio.

'TAC Three reports a direct hit on the second hydrofoil, sir.'

'Good work, Sergeant! Send them our thanks,' said Reynard. 'By the way, does anyone know how to fly a Skyraptor?'

'Flight here, sir. Our controls are still locked. We're hovering well at the moment, but I don't know for how much longer.'

'I thought I ordered you to abandon ship?' said Reynard.

'Say again, sir? Your signal's breaking up.'

****

Rusham increased their speed and skimmed a couple of waves, before hauling the TAC into level flight.

'How are you doing back there?'

'I'm okay,' said Sean, relieved to be on board after their sharp descent.

He sheltered behind Rusham to catch his breath and glanced at the sea below. It seemed calm enough, but he was not keen on falling into the cold water, even with his life vest on. He gripped the TAC and kept his head down.

'We've nearly reached our target, Sean. I'll give you a countdown. When I get to 'one' pull the trigger, understood?'

'Got it,' said Sean, smirking to himself.

Why was Rusham making so much fuss about pulling a trigger? He had fired loads of things at funfairs and arcades.

Rising from the ocean like a gigantic tornado, the waterspout soon dominated their field of vision. It seemed to defy gravity, and the noise it made was deafening. Sean felt himself shiver.

Rusham slowed and kept one hand on the TAC's throttle.

'Are you ready, Sean?'

'Yes.'

'Standby. In three, two, one, fire!' said Rusham.

Sean unclipped himself and leaned forwards. He gripped the Matteract's stock in his left hand and pulled the trigger with his right. As he did so, his left shoulder knocked against the weapon. Fortunately, the mounting held firm or Rusham would literally have lost her head.

'Come on, Sean!' said Rusham, as the spiralling water loomed ever closer.

With seconds to spare, the Matteract lit up and hummed. Sean strained against the recoil and tried to clip himself back on. However, he missed the D-ring and twisted sideways. Ahead of them, anti-matter struck seawater and vaporised a tunnel through the vortex. Rusham accelerated through the opening, and they swept through a cloud of steam, which covered Sean's visor in condensation.

The light inside the waterspout was eerie, and it rumbled like thunder. Sean gripped his legs tight around the TAC's body. He tried to lean forwards, but Rusham banked right and began to circle the platform. Again off balance, Sean thrust his tether in search of the D-ring. And missed.

'Get on there!' he cried.

'I'm trying,' said Rusham. 'Hold on.'

Sean panicked and grabbed the Matteract. He steadied himself and wiped his visor with a gloved hand.

'Come on,' he growled, through gritted teeth.

'Keep your hair on,' said Rusham, steering sharply to their left.

Unseen by his eyes, the tether leapt from Sean's hand and connected itself to the D-ring. He jolted forwards and gasped for air. The TAC spiralled down to the main deck. A mangled tower jutted out in front of them, and Rusham steered wide to avoid it.

'Slow down!' said Sean.

'You don't say?' said Rusham, jabbing at the controls in desperation.

They slowed a little, but their momentum was against them. They took a steep dive towards the main deck and headed straight for a large viewing deck.

'Brace yourself!' said Rusham.

The TAC broke through the remains of a domed roof. Its left wing cut through a window frame in a shower of sparks, slowing them for a moment. However, they ploughed on towards the floor. At the last second, Rusham raised the TAC's nose, and they struck the deck, bouncing and skidding. Their right wing caught a row of desks and dragged furniture along with them. They gouged a screeching path across the floor and began to spin. Rusham cut the engine and discharged a parachute. A tangle of cord and half-deployed material caught on a fallen girder. Sean prayed they would stop before they hit the far wall. The TAC swung on the cord and swerved left. It crashed through a door and came to rest wedged between the balustrades of a staircase.

Sean slumped forwards and felt sick.

'Nice landing,' he muttered.

'One of my best,' said Rusham.

While they recovered, Sean considered what they had done. For all they knew, Krankhausen had an army on board, and they had crashed right into the middle of his base. He shuddered at the thought.

'Hey! Over here!' cried a distant voice.

'Did you hear that?' said Rusham.

'What?' said Sean, unmoved.

Rusham slid off the TAC and reached for her blaster.

'Stay here, Sean. If I don't come back, find somewhere to hide until help comes.'

'It's okay,' said Sean, 'I think they're leaving.'

Rusham rolled her eyes.

'Yeah, right.'

She crept out into the main deck, leaving Sean to unclip himself.

Easing herself around a broken door frame, Rusham scanned the deck. Satisfied it was clear, she tiptoed around debris and trod on some broken glass.

'Crack!'

'Kuso!' she whispered.

'Who's there?' said a man's voice.

Rusham knelt behind a large, potted palm tree and surveyed the room. It was a vast space, littered with splinters of glass. The voice came from behind a bank of shattered computer screens.

'Can you cut me down?'

Rusham inched closer and took refuge behind a pile of upended furniture. It was probably a trick, she reasoned.

'Please hurry!'

Rusham switched her blaster to stun and crept towards the voice. Wreckage was piled on the deck, and she used it as cover until the stranger was in full sight.

'Don't rush, I've got all the time in the world.'

Convinced she was being watched, Rusham surveyed the room with her field glasses. Beside a rack of equipment stood a thickset man with an ugly face and thinning hair. He was tied to some wall brackets, and his wrists were purple. Rusham aimed for his torso and fired, knocking him out with a single shot. She crouched and listened. Apart from the thundering water outside, there were no sounds of any movement. Rusham inched forwards and checked the stranger's limbs. Whoever he was, he was bound securely by his hands and wrists. Krankhausen had left him to his fate but why?

'Wake up,' said Rusham, slapping the man's face.

'What?' he said, still groggy.

Rusham tried again, and this time he came around.

'Who are you?'

'Never mind. Where's Krankhausen?' said Rusham.

'Who?'

'Your boss?'

'I don't know what you're talking about.'

Rusham sighed. She would need a mind probe for this one. He was either stubborn or stupid. She tried a different tack and waved the blaster in front of his face.

'Why has Krankhausen left you dangling here like a piece of meat?'

'I upset him, I guess,' said the stranger. 'Cut me down, will you?'

Rusham shook her head.

'No way. I know where you've been.'

The stranger gestured towards the outer deck.

'Have you *seen* what's happening?'

There was an even louder roar outside. Rusham turned and watched the upper lip of the vortex fold in on itself. The weight of the falling water became a huge wave surging towards them.

'I'd hold on to something if I were you.'

'Sean?' said Rusham, sprinting back across the deck. 'Sean! Grab hold of something! There's a wave coming!' she screamed at the top of her lungs.

CHAPTER 17: CODE 96

Cuthbertson panted and wheezed up the final flight of stairs, determined to reach his office.

'Ayres, what's going on down there?'

'We've had a gas explosion in the basement, sir. At least four men are hurt. We managed to shut-off the mains, or it would have been much worse.'

'Good grief!' said Cuthbertson. 'And where's Jenkins?'

'We're not sure, sir. We spotted him climbing a lift shaft before the explosion, and we're searching the building.'

'Find him and take him down, Captain. Keep me posted.'

'Will do, sir.'

Cuthbertson drew his blaster and selected rapid fire. If Jenkins was still on the loose, he could be anywhere. Cuthbertson reasoned his state-of-the-art blaster would be more than a match for him.

****

Seawater crashed in through a shattered viewing gallery and carried a mass of debris into Krankhausen's base. Rusham clambered onto some furniture and was carried upwards by the rising water. Powerless to help, she clung to some floating debris and was buffeted ever higher by the incoming waves. Eventually, the surge died down and a strong under-current took over, dragging everything with it. Rusham watched desks and tables disappear from view, pulled by the force of the retreating water. Her own improvised raft was sure to follow, and she looked around for a means of escape.

'I'm sorry, Sean!' she cried 'Why did I ever get you into this?'

****

Reynard returned to the flight deck.

'Captain, we have our controls back,' said Flight.

'Excellent, take us to a safe height,' said Reynard.

'But the cargo doors are still locked open, sir.'

'Never mind, take us as high as you can,' said Reynard.

Skyraptor-one rose and circled the remains of Krankhausen's base. Reynard studied the waterspout and noticed life rafts scattered across the sea. Suddenly, the vortex collapsed, and several enormous waves rolled towards them.

'By Ze'us! Warn Deuce and the assault teams they have some heavy surf coming their way.'

'Yes, sir. And we have an incoming message from HQ.'

'Go ahead,' said Reynard.

'Imperative you stop Krankhausen. Use any means necessary. Keep Sean Yeager safe. Recovery craft will arrive soon. Code 96 authorised. Signed, Cassius Olandis.'

Reynard shuddered, this was the first time he had ever received a direct order from the Founder. It also meant the Founder was aware of their mission status, which was worrying.

'Right, our orders are clear,' said Reynard. 'But where *is* Sean Yeager?'

'With Agent Rusham, somewhere on that platform,' said Clavity, returning to the flight deck.

Reynard shook his head in disbelief.

'Unbelievable! Then we need to rescue them. Stand-by for recovery work, everyone.'

'But we only have our flight crew left, sir,' said Weapons. 'Everyone else is in the water.'

****

Cuthbertson stopped a short distance from his private suite. Something was wrong. He had met no commandos along the corridor, and there was a light shining from his office. He edged nearer and noticed his office door was hanging in charred pieces from its hinges. Cuthbertson crept towards the doorway and listened. A faint tapping echoed from inside his office. Someone was using his computer. Cuthbertson felt his stomach churn. Jenkins had access to restricted files, which meant he was able to log in to almost any computer. He began to feel sick. Why had he not realised this before?

'By De'us, he's found the auto-destruct codes!' he muttered.

Cuthbertson took some slow breaths to calm himself. If Jenkins succeeded, the whole base would be molten within minutes. He paused to send an SOS message and realised it would take too long for help to arrive. It was up to him to stop Jenkins or thousands of lives would be lost, including his own. He thought about his family and dogs before leaping into action. It was now or never.

'Jenkins!' he cried, charging into his office and firing at the desk.

A screen exploded and blaster bolts hit the walls and carpet. Jenkins was taken by surprise and ducked, leaving his weapon on the desktop.

'You're too late, Brigadier! Your security is a joke!'

'Give it up, Jenkins, or I'll secure you in a coffin!' said Cuthbertson, crouching beside a table and waiting for his weapon to recharge.

Jenkins reached for his blaster and fired with his head still under the desk. Shots hit the walls, pictures, and ornaments. By chance, one struck Cuthbertson's right arm and passed straight through.

'Argh!'

Cuthbertson took cover behind a leather armchair, one of three in his prized collection.

'You'll pay for what you've done!' said Jenkins and peppered all the chairs with blaster bolts.

Cuthbertson lay as flat as he could on the carpet and used his weaker left hand to hold his blaster. His right arm throbbed and brought tears to his eyes. Shots thudded through the chairs above him and ripped holes in the walls. He noticed his weapon had at last recharged. If he was lucky, he would have one last chance. He crawled forwards and aimed at knee height below the desk. His blaster erupted, releasing six shots within milliseconds. The first sent splinters flying into the air. The second hit Jenkins' weapon and wrenched it from his grasp. The third went through the computer screen and the rest threw Jenkins, backwards.

'Ahh!' he screamed.

Cuthbertson approached and peered around the shattered desk from a safe distance. Jenkins lay on his back and started to wheeze. He watched in horror as Jenkins' body began to split apart. His trunk opened to reveal squid-like creatures that sprang out and leapt across the room. Cuthbertson backed away and shook his blaster, willing it to recharge.

****

A pale man in dark glasses ranted at a bank of screens in a cramped submarine.

'Make them attack,' said Deveraux.

'I'm transmitting your orders now, master,' said Seventy-one, his underling.

The two figures watched Cuthbertson crouch and aim his weapon. They zoomed in with another camera and filled a second screen with Cuthbertson's anxious face.

'Detonate the first bio-bot!' said Deveraux.

'It will be done, master.'

They watched a squid-like creature explode, sending liquid and gases towards Cuthbertson's body. At the last moment, Cuthbertson turned his back and took the impact on his jacket.

'We have him. Detonate the second!' said Deveraux.

'Priming, master,' said Seventy-one.

In the background, two commandos raced into the room and fired their weapons. A moment later, the screen crackled and went blank.

'We've lost contact with our bio-bots, master.'

'Sha'biosh!' cried Deveraux, taking off his shades to reveal two burning red eyes. 'I tire of this failure. Head for deep water and prepare our prisoner for neural manipulation.'

'Yes, master, it will be done,' said Seventy-one, leaving the room.

****

Reynard watched the tidal waves subside and breathed a sigh of relief. A battered collection of life rafts rode out the last ripples. No doubt they were soaking, but at least they were still alive. He touched his neckpiece.

'Sergeant, are you ready?'

'Yes, sir. TAC Five is fuelled and ready to fly.'

'Okay, Flight, let's fish out our rescue party. Sergeant, prepare to welcome our lucky volunteers aboard.'

'Yes, sir, I'm preparing the cargo nets now.'

'Captain, we have messages from three recovery craft heading our way,' said Comms.

'At last!' said Reynard. 'Tell them to get here as soon as possible.'

'Yes, sir.'

Skyraptor-one approached a cluster of life rafts and hovered above them. Briggs lowered cargo nets into the sea and helped four sodden commandos to haul themselves onto the loading ramp.

'Enjoy your swim, lads?'

'Very refreshing, Sarge,' said a burly commando, who was dripping from head to toe.

'Right, lads, Captain Reynard needs us to get over there and finish our mission.'

'We've tried that already, Sarge. It was a complete wash-out,' said another commando.

'Seriously, lads, we have a gutsy young lady and lad on that heap. Heaven knows if they're alive or dead, but they need our help. Let's show them what Sigma Force can do.'

'Yes, sir!' said the four commandos together.

'Tool up, and prepare for an abseil drop,' said Briggs. 'And this time I'm coming with you.'

The commandos squelched through the Skyraptor in search of weapons and equipment. They raided every storage compartment they could find and assembled a pile of helmets, gloves, dry clothes, and sidearms.

'Not exactly standard issue, but it will have to do,' said Briggs.

They were joined by Reynard and stood to attention.

'Your mission, gentlemen, is to rescue Agent Rusham and Sean Yeager. After that, clear Krankhausen's base of enemy personnel, weapons and Foundation equipment. Any questions?'

'What about the hostiles, sir?' said a commando.

'Take them prisoner if you can. But if they put up a fight, you're authorised to use lethal force,' said Reynard, nodding to Briggs.

'Get ready, lads. Drop time is in five minutes.'

Briggs took Reynard to one side.

'What are your plans for the spare TAC, Captain?'

'I'll come and get you if you're caught in a fire-fight,' said Reynard.

'Very good, sir,' said Briggs.

****

Sean sat dazed for a few minutes. His TAC was wedged at an awkward angle, and he needed time to recover after their crash landing. He heard a deafening roar of water and someone shouting. It sounded like Rusham, but her voice was too faint to carry above the din. He guessed that either way it was bad news and tried to free himself by unclipping his tether. He tugged it in all directions, but it refused to budge. The metal clip was fused solid, and he was chained to the TAC.

Over his shoulder, he noticed seawater stream around the broken door. It carried pieces of broken furniture, which began to gather behind the TAC. Water cascaded downstairs in a trickle, which quickly became a flood. It grew more and more powerful until it filled the lower stairwell. Sean felt the TAC rock beneath him, and the strong current began to turn it around by its tail. Cold seawater splashed onto his sneakers, and he lifted his feet clear of the water line.

While he sat pinned to his seat, a long forgotten memory flashed into Sean's mind. He was at the seaside hunting for crabs in a tidal pool. He stumbled and wedged his right foot between two jagged rocks near the water's edge. He felt a cold tide wash over his socks and tried to move, but his shoe was stuck tight. In a panic, he cried out for help. A familiar man approached, though he could not remember his face. The man reached into the foaming water and untied his shoelace, releasing his foot. At once, Sean felt a sense of relief as he was carried away from the rocks holding a dripping pair of shoes and socks.

'That's it!' thought Sean. What was it his mum always told him? Think laterally.'

Rusham had done a great job of tightening his life vest, but, within a few seconds, Sean had unbuckled it. He pulled it off and was free. It was just as well because the water was now almost up to his seat. Sean discarded the lifejacket and clambered along the middle of the TAC on his hands and knees. He reached the nose cone and caught hold of the stair rail. By levering himself sideways, he jumped across onto a dry step. He hurried up the first few flights and dared not look back until he reached a safe height. Below him, the TAC groaned and screeched before sliding into the stairwell.

'That was close,' he whispered. 'I hope Rusham's okay.'

Sean climbed to a landing and listened. Apart from the roaring water and the creaking of metal, there was nothing. There were no voices and no footsteps.

'Right, what have you done with my Dreampad?' he said.

Sean scaled a flight of stairs and reached an upper floor. A light shone from a half-open doorway, and he inched forwards to investigate. He entered a short corridor which led to a set of open glass doors. He slipped through an airlock and entered a brilliant white room with curved walls. Its windows were darkened, and it resembled a large doctor's surgery. A smell of antiseptic hung in the air. Hairs prickled on Sean's neck, and he sensed he was not alone. An examination couch lay on its side among an array of discarded medical equipment. Sean tiptoed around them.

From an office on his left came a muffled sound. He stopped dead in his tracks, his pulse racing, and ducked behind an overturned cabinet.

'Hungry,' said a child-like voice.

A tall, hunched figure staggered across the room and began to pick at some fallen equipment. It wore grey overalls and had a full head of brown hair with smooth, flushed skin. Its face was full and round, like a baby's, and it waddled uncertainly.

'Want food,' said the gigantic man-child, shuffling into the office.

Sean hurried to another hiding place and peered around a medical trolley. He spotted two figures in the office and noticed they were arguing. The second figure was dressed all in black and appeared to be rifling through cupboards and drawers. Its eyes flashed red. The giant pestered it and was shoved out of the way. Red-eyes continued its search.

'Hungry!' cried the giant.

Red-eyes turned and fired two darts at its tormenter, one of which struck an arm or shoulder.

'Hurts! Hurts!' cried the giant and hobbled out of the office.

Red-eyes packed a medical bag and emerged from the doorway. It scanned the room, and its eyes glistened like lasers. Sean dropped to his knees and hid. He waited. Footsteps crossed the room. They paused.

'Give me!' cried the giant.

There was a crash like someone falling onto the floor and

142

a groan. It was followed by more footsteps, which became quieter and quieter. Sean rose and edged around the trolley. The man-child lay on its side mewling, but there was no sign of red-eyes.

'What are they hiding in *there*?' thought Sean.

He stole across the room and hurried inside the office. It was a mess. Papers were strewn all over the floor and drawers were upended. Sean noticed an upturned lamp and a bowl of fruit on a desk. Something colourful caught his eye. It was a partly concealed comic. He approached the desk and uncovered a familiar-looking page.

'Rise of the Ultrabulous One!' he muttered.

Sean rolled it up and tucked it inside his jacket. He scoured the office for his Dreampad, turning over piles of paper and sifting through the discarded contents of drawers.

'Give food!' cried the giant.

Sean turned around. The man-child stood in the doorway. It had a dart stuck in its arm and reached out a hand towards him.

'Who you?' slobbered the giant, its jaws wide open.

It appeared to have tiny teeth and spoke like an overgrown toddler. Sean looked around for something he could use to defend himself. Apart from the lamp, there was nothing.

'Want food,' said the creature, staring into Sean's eyes. 'Give me!' it cried, waving its fist.

The giant bounded closer, and Sean backed away behind the desk. He kept the creature at arm's length, but his escape route was blocked. Every time he darted to one side of the desk, the man-child moved to block his path. It pounded a fist on the desktop.

'Hungry!'

'The fruit bowl,' thought Sean. 'I wonder?'

He lunged and grabbed it before backing away from the creature. It was a thin, wooden dish containing a handful of apples and a battered-looking orange.

'Here,' said Sean, waving an apple. 'What's this?'

The giant began to slobber and gazed at the fruit with

wide eyes.

'Give me.'

Sean held the apple out in front of him and threw it out of the office door.

'Fetch!'

The creature grunted and scampered after it, bouncing off the doorframe on its way out. Sean took a deep sigh and continued his search.

'It has to be here somewhere!'

While rummaging through a pile of papers, he came across a photograph of a young man stapled to a list of names. The face seemed familiar, and he read his own name and address on a printed sheet. At the top of the page was a title which read: 'Foundation Priority-one Subjects.'

'That's Dad,' whispered Sean. 'It has to be.'

A shuffling sound disturbed his thoughts.

'Need more!'

Sean hurried back to the desk and selected an orange. This time, the creature caught it in mid-air and bit straight into its peel.

'Yuck! Not like!' it cried and threw the orange onto the floor.

To buy himself some more time, Sean hurled another apple over the giant's shoulder. He returned to the photograph and folded it away inside a pocket. He was about to search the last drawer when a fog gripped his mind. A pair of dark eyes fixed on his own, and his thoughts clouded over.

'Feel my pain,' said a deep, soulless voice.

A blinding ache spread through Sean's head. He staggered behind the desk and slumped into a chair. He was vaguely aware of his hands typing, while his eyes glazed over in a red mist.

'Confirm self-destruct timing,' intoned the computer.

Sean's hand reached for a mouse and clicked a button.

'Self-destruct in five minutes. Confirm your selection.'

The dark eyes returned, and a piercing sensation stung the back of his eyes.

'No!' cried Sean.

His hand reached for the 'enter' button.

'Need more!'

Sean felt himself being dragged out of the chair and across the desk. He fell onto the floor. His eyes cleared, and he found the giant looming over him, its face flushed with rage.

'Still hungry!'

Sean looked around for the fruit bowl. It lay several feet away, upside-down and out of reach. The last apple was nowhere to be seen.

'There! Look!' said Sean, pointing.

The giant followed his gaze and spotted the fruit bowl. It lumbered towards it. While the creature tried to pick it up, Sean rolled onto his side and crawled away. He reached the doorway and staggered to his feet.

'Need more!' cried the giant.

'Sean picked up a discarded metal tray and ran for his life. He had almost reached the outermost door when the giant caught him by his jacket. He lashed out with the tray and beat it away howling. It was a pathetic sight, but Sean was determined not to be on the menu.

'Find something else to eat!'

The creature hauled itself up and snarled in his direction.

CHAPTER 18: HOME TRUTHS

Sean raced back to the staircase, pursued by the now enraged creature. He considered his options. He could climb higher in the hope of hiding on an upper deck or take his chances in the floodwater below. Something told him swimming was a better choice, and Sean descended as fast as he could. He raced down the stairs, half sliding on the handrail, and reached the lower deck. The water level had subsided, although the stairwell was still flooded. Sean managed to wade across the landing. Up to his knees in cold seawater, he headed for the main deck. The giant followed but hesitated at the water's edge.

'Hungry! Want food!'

From a safe distance, Sean watched the creature dip a bare foot in the water. It flinched.

'Cold!'

It took a faltering step, slipped and fell. Sean hoped the creature would be frightened, but it leapt up again, spluttering and shaking its head. It reminded him of a freakish pet and not the kind you would want to take home.

The main deck was now peaceful. Water dripped from the walls, and most of the furniture had gone. Sean headed for the viewing gallery, in the hope of finding a way out. Wading through the flood was hard work, and he was soon out of breath.

'It's gaining on you! Run!' cried a voice from above.

Sean looked up and saw Rusham nestled on a roof girder.

'Can't you shoot it?' he cried.

Rusham shook her head and turned out her pockets.

'I've lost my blaster. Head for the outer deck!'

The creature waded towards him, its hands stretched out.

'Want food now!'

'Up here, you big gorilla!' cried Rusham.

The giant stopped for a moment, unsure of what to do.

'Here, catch!' said Rusham, snapping a flare stick and letting it go.

It landed in the water and blazed a brilliant red. The creature stepped back, covered its face and screamed. The flare hissed and flashed, before burning out and submerging. In the meantime, Sean took refuge behind a heap of fallen metalwork and looked around. His exit was blocked by debris piled up on the inside of the viewing deck.

A familiar howl of engines echoed around them.

'Go, team! Go!' cried a voice.

Several black lines fell from the sky and splashed into the water. Seconds later, four commandos arrived at speed and stopped just above the waterline to unclip themselves.

'Need food!' said the creature, wading towards the nearest.

It was stopped in its tracks by a stun-shot and fell to its knees.

'Where's, Sean?' said Briggs, eyeing Rusham with a bemused look.

'He's over here!' cried a commando.

Briggs detached a grappling hook and line from his webbing and threw it over Rusham's girder. It looped in the air, caught the metal spar and span around it.

'Come on down, m'lady, we've no time to hang around. I take it you can abseil?'

Rusham grunted and began to climb down the girder.

'How do you think I got up here?' she said.

Meanwhile, Sean accepted a commando's help and allowed himself to be fitted into a harness.

'But what about my Dreampad?'

'My job is to keep you alive, son,' said the commando, giving a thumbs-up. 'Happy landings.'

Sean felt the harness dig into his body, and in a moment he was weightless. He passed through the remains of the damaged roof and swayed above Krankhausen's base. Eager hands hauled him on board Skyraptor-one and helped him to his feet on the cargo ramp. Sean stepped out of the harness and was surprised to be hugged by Major Clavity.

'Welcome back, big guy. I'm glad to see you in one piece.'

Sean took a step back.

'Yeah, okay. Steady.'

****

Cuthbertson was badly hurt, but thanks to medication he only felt a little light-headed. He sat in a blue medical gown on the edge of a hospital bed.

'I just need to make a quick call, Doctor. I won't be long.'

The doctor smiled and wrote some notes on a clipboard. He gestured to a nurse who nodded and inspected an injector cartridge. Cuthbertson dialled a number.

'Reynard here, sir. How can I help you?'

'What's your mission status, Captain?'

'We've recovered Rusham and Yeager and we've searched Krankhausen's base.'

'Any sign of him?'

'None, sir. But we've taken two prisoners.'

'And have you found the Matteract?'

'No, sir, there's no trace of it.'

'Okay, Captain, carry out Code 96. We don't want any awkward questions from our international partners.'

'Right away, sir. We're charging up the cannons now. By the way, the recovery craft have arrived, and they've started to lift Deuce.'

'Very good, Captain. Carry on. Over and out.'

As he spoke, the nurse touched the injector cartridge to his neck, and Cuthbertson folded sideways onto the bed. The doctor sighed and removed the phone from Cuthbertson's grasp, before handing it to the nurse.

'Sleep well, Brigadier,' he said, lifting Cuthbertson's legs onto the bed.

Cuthbertson lay in the Foundation Medical Centre for several days. His shoulder and neck were heavily bandaged, and he slept off the effects of a major operation. Two strangers dressed as orderlies entered his private room. They scanned from floor to ceiling and closed the blinds. Once they were sure everything was in order, one of them spoke into his neckpiece. The men drew weapons from inside their coats and took up positions beside the door and bed. They were joined by a tall, slim figure dressed in a grey trench coat. The figure approached the bed and put his hands gently on either side of Cuthbertson's temples. He closed his pale grey eyes as if meditating.

'Wake,' he whispered.

Cuthbertson stirred and sat upright.

'I wasn't expecting you, sir,' said Cuthbertson, becoming agitated.

'Relax, Henry. You can call me Cassius. I hear you've had a challenging couple of days?'

'I can only apologise, sir.'

Cassius Olandis walked slowly around the bed and pulled up a plastic chair. As he did so, he studied Cuthbertson's face and smiled. He leaned towards a vase of flowers and took in their scent.

'Why are you so worried, Henry?'

Cuthbertson released a deep breath.

'It's all been such a mess, sir. What with the damage and everything.'

'Yes, I can remember some dark days. April 1815 and June 1908 were particularly difficult. We live in troubled times, Henry,' said Olandis.

'Are you relieving me of command?' said Cuthbertson.

'Good grief no, Henry! I didn't recruit you from the Army to drop you at the first sign of trouble,' said Olandis. 'Your team has done remarkably well in the circumstances.'

Cuthbertson looked confused. Krankhausen had escaped, a Matteract was lost, and the Foundation's headquarters had been seriously damaged. How could his team possibly have done well? He was unsure whether to believe his ears or to resign on the spot.

'My dear, Henry, it is I who should be apologising. And I think I owe you an explanation,' said Olandis.

Cuthbertson was uncertain what to say. Instead, he waited for Olandis to speak.

'Several months ago, we were approached by a number of governments and asked to shut down Krankhausen's operation. Since we prefer to keep our partners on good terms, we agreed.'

Cuthbertson's eyes widened. He knew the Foundation cooperated with governments around the world, but why had he not been informed?

'So we laid some bait to expose Krankhausen.'

'Sean Yeager?' said Cuthbertson.

'Actually, no, it was Jenkins.'

Cuthbertson was surprised.

'So why have we been protecting the Yeager boy all this time?'

Olandis was silent for a moment as if choosing his words. He glanced at the ceiling and drew a long breath.

'Because, Henry, Sean is an investment. One day he'll join the Foundation, and we must do everything we can to protect our future generations.'

'I see,' said Cuthbertson, unconvinced. 'But what did Krankhausen want from Jenkins?'

'Information, or so we thought. However, it appears our enemies are far more cunning than we anticipated.'

Cuthbertson was taken aback. Had his entire organisation been put at risk to catch only *one* criminal?

'Ah, my dear Henry, I do believe you're teasing me,' said Olandis.

'About what?' said Cuthbertson, feigning innocence.

'Surely you already know why we took these risks?'

Cuthbertson felt stunned.

'I do?'

Olandis poured a cup of water, and Cuthbertson gratefully accepted it.

'Simply put, Henry, we have enemies,' said Olandis. 'And

we've had them for many years.'

Cuthbertson spluttered water onto his bed sheets.

'Krankhausen? We should have caught him years ago.'

Olandis shook his head.

'We tracked a craft leaving Krankhausen's base; it was almost certainly Darius Deveraux.'

'Who?' said Cuthbertson, bemused.

'Darius Deveraux is possibly the richest and most dangerous man on this planet.'

Cuthbertson was dumbfounded.

'But where's Krankhausen?'

'Somewhere deep underwater, if he's still alive. We lost track of Deveraux's submarine soon after it left Krankhausen's base.'

Cuthbertson tried to stifle a yawn. Instead, his eyes watered. He felt as if his whole world had collapsed around him and the past few days had been a bad dream.

'I can see you need rest, Henry. We can talk again later,' said Olandis, rising from his chair. 'By the way, I'll be borrowing Major Clavity for a few months. Oh, and Captain Reynard sends his regards.'

Cuthbertson shrugged at the prospect of losing Clavity. He would be glad if Clavity left the Foundation altogether. Reynard, on the other hand, was a good man.

'And one last thing, we need to reward Agent Rusham,' said Olandis, putting his chair back in place.

'What for? She put the entire mission at risk.'

'Henry, if it were not for her actions we would have lost Sigma Force.'

Olandis turned and walked towards the door followed by his bodyguards.

'Goodbye, Henry, I wish you a speedy recovery. Now, rest.'

Cuthbertson's eyes closed, and he slumped into a deep and relaxing sleep.

****

On Skyraptor-one the mood was buoyant. A weary crew looked forward to seeing their families again. However, Sean was unusually quiet.

'So much for keeping you safe, Sean. Any chance of you staying at home next time?' said Clavity.

Sean shook his head.

'It's boring at home.'

'What I don't understand is where Krankhausen disappeared to,' said Rusham, stretching her right arm as high as it would allow.

Clavity shrugged and looked to Sean.

'What do you think?'

Sean stared blankly into space. He was wary of being admonished and was still angry about losing his Dreampad.

'Underwater, presumably?' said Clavity.

Sean nodded and looked out of the cabin window.

'I hear you picked up a pet monster, Sean?' said Clavity. 'Some kind of mutant?'

'Don't tease him,' said Rusham. 'He's been through a lot today.'

'It's not his fault,' said Sean. 'He didn't ask to be made. They weren't feeding him properly, that's all.'

'Speaking of which,' said Clavity, passing across two foil trays of rations. 'Here you go. I bet you could eat a horse?'

Sean took the food and smiled, but Rusham raised her eyebrows in disgust.

'Or a mushroom, if you prefer?' said Clavity. 'Anyway, what happened to the other prisoner?'

'He's in the brig,' said Rusham. 'But he's not talking.'

'Any idea who he is?'

'No, but I think Krankhausen left him behind for a reason,' said Rusham.

'He's dangerous,' said Sean.

'All the more reason to bring him back with us for questioning,' said Clavity.

'Orders are orders, Major. Surely you of all people know

that?' said Rusham. 'But I still don't understand how we escaped from that platform.'

'I'm just glad you're both back in one piece,' said Clavity.

Sean finished his mouthful and licked his lips.

'They only wanted Krankhausen and something from the laboratory.'

'Perhaps they couldn't control the waterspout and attack us at the same time?' said Clavity.

Rusham frowned.

'More likely, they saw the recovery ships and fled. I think we just got lucky.'

'Either way, you're both heroes,' said Clavity.

'Tell that to Reynard,' said Rusham. 'He won't even look me in the eye.'

If this was how heroes felt, Sean was not interested. All he wanted was to return home and get some sleep. He hoped his mother would buy him a new Dreampad, if he played his cards right. However, the rest of his belongings were irreplaceable. He checked the comic tucked away inside his jacket and felt a sense of relief. At least he still had one of the comics his father had left him.

Agent Rusham looked quizzical.

'Don't worry about it; he'll come around,' said Clavity. 'And Reynard still owes you a dinner, doesn't he?'

Rusham scowled.

****

Professor Quark hobbled into Cuthbertson's private ward carrying a bottle in his hand. Cuthbertson noticed Quark's nose and chin were covered in plasters.

'What happened to you, Professor?'

'I tried balancing a fire door on my face. I wouldn't recommend it as a party trick.'

Cuthbertson laughed.

'So who's running things while I'm shackled in here?'

'Captain Ayres and Agent Lee I believe,' said Quark. 'I

154

don't think we'll be hearing wedding bells anytime soon, however.'

Cuthbertson frowned.

'It's okay, Henry, I'm keeping an eye on them,' said Quark, with a grin.

Cuthbertson noticed the bottle in Quark's hand and nodded mischievously.

'I offer a trade,' said Quark. 'This fine vintage for a substantially increased budget.'

'You strike a hard bargain, Professor. I'll see what I can do,' said Cuthbertson, reaching for a cup. 'By the way, what in heaven's name happened to Jenkins?'

Quark pushed his glasses further up his plastered nose.

'That's a very good question, Henry. We're not sure.'

Cuthbertson looked surprised.

'Haven't you carried out an autopsy?'

'We've examined his remains. But to be honest, Henry, we've never seen anything like it.'

'What do you mean?'

Quark coughed to clear his throat.

'Jenkins wasn't entirely human. His body was a collection of symbiotic organisms inside a human shell.'

'Are you referring to those squid things?'

'Yes. We examined his body, but there wasn't much left of him. My guess is the squids were engineered specially to attack. Of course, one of them exploded right in front of you.'

'Exploded? How?' said Cuthbertson.

'By igniting a mixture of organic gases,' said Quark. 'By the way, we found traces of acid and venom on your uniform. You're lucky to be alive.'

Cuthbertson paled.

'Was Jenkins always carrying those creatures?'

'We don't think so. Judging by the scar tissue inside his body, we believe he was altered from the inside.'

'And he thought the Foundation had killed his sister?'

Quark nodded.

155

'Whoever did this to him needed his appearance to be unchanged. They brainwashed him and ordered him to come after you.'

Cuthbertson winced.

'Poor man.'

'Indeed.'

Cuthbertson had so many questions, but he struggled to find the right words in his drowsy condition. The effects of his operation were beginning to catch up on him.

'I expect you want to know about Sean Yeager and the prisoners?' said Quark.

'Another time, Professor. But please don't let them out of your sight?'

Quark walked to the door and offered a brief wave of his hand.

'I'll keep an eye on things,' he said. 'And I'll visit you again tomorrow.'

****

It was a few hours after touchdown, and Sean was fast asleep in the back of a chauffeur-driven limousine. Rusham sat beside him with Mrs Yeager, who was relieved to see her son again.

'Where are you taking us?' said Mrs Yeager, in a calm voice. 'I thought we were going home?'

Rusham gave a faint smile.

'The Founder insisted we move you both to a safe house. We were concerned about the burglars coming back. The Founder sends his thanks and best wishes.'

'But what about our belongings?'

'They've already been packed and moved,' said Rusham. 'I think you'll be pleasantly surprised.'

Mrs Yeager looked unconvinced as they drove along a narrow lane and approached a large, walled building and a gatehouse. A guard in plain clothes approached them and scanned the car.

'It's a hotel!' said Mrs Yeager. 'You're going to make us live in a hotel?'

Rusham smiled.

'Actually, the entire house is just for you and Sean. And your staff, of course.'

Mrs Yeager was speechless. She peered out at an elegant, stately home and glanced at Rusham, who nodded reassuringly.

'Oh, and before I forget, Major Clavity wanted Sean to have this,' said Rusham.

Mrs Yeager accepted a chunky watch.

'It's a small gift. We didn't manage to recover any of his belongings.'

'And how are you?' said Mrs Yeager, noticing Rusham's bandaged wrist.

'It's only a sprain; I'll be fine. They're promoting me to Sigma Squad.'

'Please be honest with me, are we in danger?' said Mrs Yeager, staring deep into Rusham's eyes.

Rusham gave a faint smile.

'We believe Krankhausen is dead, and the team here will protect you twenty-four hours a day. This is only a precaution, Mrs Yeager.'

Sarah Yeager nodded. It was the same well-rehearsed story she had heard many times before. But when would it end?

****

Greerbo sat on a bare mattress in an isolation cell deep inside Foundation HQ. He twitched slightly and sneezed. His head began to throb, and he lay down to rest. Visions of destruction filled his mind and he let out a groan. His body began to cramp.

CHAPTER 19: EVIDENCE

When the mind upload had finally ended, Deijan Klesus rolled over in his chair and groaned. He reached for an energy tonic and gulped it down. He felt exhausted and far too old for his punishing regime.

'Next time, 12-59, can you just show me the highlights?'

'Affirmative, those were the highlights,' said the spy-bot. 'Would you like to review more information?'

'No thanks; tell me only what I need to know.'

Klesus' brain struggled to interpret the vast amount of data he had received. He felt a migraine coming on, and he knew it would be days until his thoughts would be clear again.

'What information do you require?' said 12-59.

'Show me this unusual DNA,' said Klesus.

A holographic display filled the centre of his living quarters. In mid-air, colourful DNA molecules and clumps of broken spirals floated in three dimensions.

'We gathered data from Sean Yeager's samples,' said 12-59.

'Alviqua, display a comparison of these fragments with Aenaid DNA,' said Klesus.

A kaleidoscope of shapes traced around the spirals and staircases in front of him. The traces met and overlapped, becoming one in all but a few places.

'We have a 92% match, Deijan,' said Alviqua. 'All the unique Aenaid base pairs are present.'

Klesus rubbed his temples. In his stressed condition, it was a struggle to think straight. He drank some more tonic and considered his next question.

'Who were the parents of this subject?'

There was silence for a moment, while the sentient computer prepared its answer. Klesus took another sip of tonic. With any luck, it would either wake him or send him into a deep sleep. He didn't care which.

'We found insufficient evidence to confirm the parents of this subject,' said 12-59.

Klesus raised his eyebrows in frustration. Another useless answer.

'Show me the design of this Matteract.'

A blueprint appeared alongside an image of a Matteract, which opened to reveal its working parts in three dimensions. Klesus was impressed.

'And who invented this device?'

'We found no evidence to confirm the inventor,' said 12-59.

'Oh, come on!' said Klesus. 'What have you being doing all this time?'

'Please clarify your question,' said 12-59.

'Forget it,' said Klesus. 'Confirm the origins of the lifeform known as Darius Deveraux.'

'Darius Deveraux is confirmed as a hybrid humanoid.'

'Hybrid from what sources?' said Klesus.

'A human and an unknown life form,' said 12-59.

'Let me guess; you found insufficient evidence to confirm the other life form?'

'Affirmative,' said 12-59.

Klesus sighed. It was clear something unusual was happening on Terra Prime, but obtaining reliable facts about the anomalies was proving difficult. It reminded him of reading ancient Terran newspapers when he was a student. They were full of half-truths, distractions and outright lies. At the time, it occurred to him that Terrans were the most accomplished liars in the galaxy, which was quite an achievement given the youthfulness of their race.

'Take a wild guess, 12-59. What other life form gave genes to this Darius Deveraux?'

'We have insufficient evidence to determine…'

'I see,' said Klesus. 'So why didn't you take samples of Deveraux's DNA?'

'Deijan, we tried to obtain samples, but our probe was detected and destroyed,' said Alviqua.

This was a puzzling situation. It was unusual for Aenaid probes to be detected, let alone destroyed.

'Alviqua, I have made my decision, please carry out my orders.'

'I am ready to receive your orders, Deijan,' intoned the computer.

'Send another scout ship to Terra Prime. If it finds an Aenaid colony there, I want them brought back to Aenathen Omega for debriefing. And find the commander of the first scout ship. I want to know exactly what happened to his mission.'

Alviqua considered his orders for several long seconds.

'It will be done, Deijan.'

'I also want to know more about this Darius Deveraux and the inventor of the Matteract.'

'Thank you for your orders, Deijan. It will be done,' said Alviqua.

Klesus staggered to his sleeping quarters. He hoped to relax for at least a few hours.

'Sentients!' he muttered, his mind still racing.

Klesus reached for another glass of tonic. In his fragile heart, he knew it would not be long until he was woken again.

The End

(of the first adventure)

Read on for an excerpt from:

Sean Yeager Hunters Hunted

Thank you for reading this story. We hope you have enjoyed it. If you have, please tell your friends and family. **Please post a review on Amazon, Goodreads or a similar site. They really help other readers to discover Sean Yeager and his adventures**

Sean Yeager *continues his quest for answers in Hunters Hunted. Rumour has it, Sean meets a new friend and goes in search of a mysterious treasure, while Darius Deveraux carries out his evil plan. But you didn't hear anything from us, okay?*

For more information *about Sean Yeager's world visit the website at:*

www.SeanYeager.com

Titles in sequence:
Sean Yeager and the DNA Thief
Sean Yeager Hunters Hunted
Sean Yeager Claws of Time
Sean Yeager Mortal Thread

Hughes joined a four-lane road lined by trees. Vehicles passed on either side, but the traffic was light for a Saturday morning.

'Where to now?'

'Turn right at the end,' said Stafford. 'The mall is just a few blocks away.'

Sean felt a shiver run through his spine.

'Someone's following us.'

'Yeah, about half of Yeatsford,' said Hughes.

'There's nothing on our scope,' said Stafford.

A car exploded on their left and careered into the air. Hughes swerved to avoid it and accelerated away. Stafford spotted three flying shapes on the rearview camera. They skimmed above the traffic and fired a volley of energy bolts.

'Hostiles detected. Take evasive action,' said Pegasus.

'Burn rubber!' said Stafford.

'I'm trying,' said Hughes.

'Hurry, man. They're gaining.'

'Is there any chance of you shooting back?' said Hughes.

'Pegasus, activate manual cannons,' said Stafford, pulling a control pad from the glove box.

Hughes gunned the engine and weaved around slower traffic. Pegasus raced past a speed camera, which flashed for a second before bursting into flames.

'Darn it!' said Stafford.

'You sure roasted that speed camera,' said Hughes.

'Never mind your speeding ticket, get us to the mall!'

Hughes took a sharp right and threw his passengers sideways. An energy bolt skimmed their roof and incinerated a nearby tree.

'Can't we just fly out of here?' said Sean.

'No,' said Stafford 'We're not allowed to fly in built-up areas.'

'Even in an emergency?' said Hughes.

'You're not trained. And I could lose my job.'

Sean glanced out of the rear window. He counted six flying craft split into two groups. Their pilots knelt forwards on small, black machines and were difficult to see against the gloomy sky.

'Boom!'

A passing van rolled onto its roof. Hughes steered around it, screeching all four wheels.

'They're gaining on us!' said Hughes.

A cannon blast from Pegasus hit one of the hostile craft. It swerved into the back of a double-decker bus, and its pilot crashed through an upstairs window. He landed face-down on a seat and lay there dazed for a moment. Meanwhile, the passengers did their best to ignore the dark-suited intruder, as if his sudden arrival was somehow a regular occurrence. A ticket inspector arrived.

'Hey, mate, have you got a ticket?'

The androbot righted itself, ran back down the aisle and jumped out of the broken window headfirst. It somersaulted in mid-air, dented a car roof and sprinted away after its colleagues.

'Young people today…' said an elderly passenger.

Pegasus accelerated around a corner and under a concrete bridge. Two hostiles had almost caught up, but they misjudged their speed. One flew over the bridge and crashed into an office block. The second scraped under the bridge and tore into a row of orange ceiling lights. Its pilot was unseated and rolled down the road, while the craft bounced and exploded.

'In there,' said Stafford, pointing at an entrance labelled: 'Staff only'.

Hughes smashed through a barrier and headed for a row of illuminated glass doors at one end of the mall.

'Where now?' said Hughes.

'Inside!' said Stafford.

Pegasus mounted a curb and skidded to a halt. As it did so, a man wearing a fluorescent bib appeared and gestured towards them.

'Hey, you can't park here! This is a staff car park!'

Stafford hauled Sean out of the car.

'I meant *through* the doors.'

'Call me squeamish, but I'm not into head-on collisions,' said Hughes, turning off the engine.

The parking attendant blocked Stafford's path and jabbed his finger at Pegasus.

'I need you to move your vehicle *this instant,* or I'm calling the police.'

Stafford brushed him aside.

'Go ahead. And while you're at it, tell the police about *them*!'

A group of androbots had gathered at the entrance to the car park, like a gang of bikers. They spread out to block the road.

'Pegasus, auto-protect system on,' said Stafford, ushering Sean towards the shopping centre.

'Armed and ready,' said Pegasus.

The parking attendant took one look at the hovering androbots and began to jab his finger in their direction. However, before he could say a word, the air was full of energy bolts and missiles. The exchange was brief and brutal. The androbots fired and missed, shattering the doors to the shopping mall. In return, Pegasus unleashed a volley of heat-seeking missiles and plasma bolts. It destroyed three androbots and numerous cars. The remaining androbots scattered and launched an aerial bombardment. Energy bolts struck Pegasus on its roof and exposed side. It was thrown against the curb and rolled over a line of concrete bollards. It smashed through a plate-glass window and came to rest lying upside down in the shopping mall. Meanwhile, the parking attendant crawled away on his hands and knees to the sound of car alarms. The staff car park resembled a war zone.

****

Quark's team were busy inspecting cars in the vehicle pound.

'Professor, they've all been sabotaged,' said a technician.

'Impossible!' said Cuthbertson, brushing Quark aside and marching past a line of vehicles.

Cuthbertson climbed into his sports car and slammed the door. He started up its engine, which gave a brief clunk and died. When he tried to get out, he discovered the door was locked tight. Enraged, Cuthbertson thumped on the driver's window and struggled to be heard. A short while later, Quark's phone rang.

'Quark here.'

'It's Cuthbertson. I'm stuck in my infernal car!'

'So, it *is* possible?'

'Get me out of here, Quark!'

'I'll be right with you, sir.'

While Cuthbertson waited to be rescued, a voice spoke on an emergency intercom channel.

'Control, this is Stafford. We are under attack! Send help immediately!'

Cuthbertson tried to join the call, but none of the car's controls would respond. He resorted to using his phone and ordered Captain Ayres to report to the vehicle pound. Meanwhile, Quark arrived with a technician.

'I'll need welding gear; we'll have to cut him out,' said the technician, hurrying away to the stores.

Ayres arrived accompanied by three burly commandos.

'Reporting as ordered, Professor. Where's the Brigadier?'

'He's on a phone conference,' said Quark. 'Follow me.'

Quark led the commandos to the far end of the car park. He opened a sliding door and switched on ceiling lights to reveal an expanse of storage space. On one side, stood a row of machines covered in heavy tarpaulins. Quark unveiled one.

'We have a team of agents caught up in a fire-fight at Yeatsford shopping centre, and I need your men to help them.'

'Sure, no problem,' said Ayres. 'Fleet can fly us over there in minutes.'

Quark shook his head.

'I wish we could. Skyraptor-one is on a mission, and Skyraptor-two is being repaired. Our Hoverlifters are too vulnerable, and our Hyperjets are on their way back from Redoubt Island.'

'What about the carpool?' said Ayres.

'Immobilized. Every single vehicle has been sabotaged,' said Quark.

'So, tell me about this...*bike*, Professor?'

'We discovered them last year in a deep storage facility.'

Ayres and his men crowded around the strange machine. It looked like a cross between a motorbike and a snowmobile, except it had no wheels. A long, swept seat met a triangular cross-section and a fluted skid ran along its underside. A flattened, conical nose and windshield protected the rider, while two exhaust grilles extended from its rear. The vehicle stood upright, covered by a thin layer of dust.

'What is it?' said Ayres.

'This is a Glidebike,' said Quark.

'And how does it work?'

'We looked for a manual in the archives. All we could find was this.'

Quark handed Ayres a frayed sheet of paper. Printed on one side was a single sentence.

'Activate the mind link by gripping the handles and placing your right thumb on the touch plate.'

Ayres eyed the machine with suspicion.

'Do we know what it's capable of?'

'Not really,' said Quark. 'We considered testing one several years ago, but it was never a priority.'

'And who's involved in this fire-fight, Professor?'

'Nine agents and one guard. The hostiles seem to be after Sean Yeager.'

'*Again?* What is it with that kid?' said Ayres, shaking his head in disbelief.

Quark tapped his nose.

'All I can tell you is that Sean Yeager is very important to our mission.'

Ayres took a deep breath and glanced at the faces of his men. They each nodded.

'Alright, we'll do it. Squad, fetch your body armour and weapons, on the double.'

'Yes, sir!' said the commandos, hurrying away.

When his men had departed, Ayres turned to Quark.

'Are these going to work, Professor?'

'Of course,' said Quark. 'All it will take is a little focus.'

****

While Hughes covered their retreat, Stafford pulled Sean through a crowd of shoppers. Alarms rang out from the far end of the shopping mall, and security staff brandishing walkie-talkies hurried to investigate. Inside the mall, shoppers milled around like herds of sheep, oblivious to the drama outside.

'In here,' said Stafford, heading for a department store.

'What's your plan?' said Hughes.

'To stay alive long enough to be rescued,' said Stafford.

'What about *them*?' said Sean, indicating the shoppers.

'Best worry about your own skin,' said Hughes. 'Come on.'

The trio entered a ground-floor cosmetics department and weaved through a maze of glitzy display cases.

'Doof!'

A shelf of perfume bottles erupted beside them, drenching customers and shop assistants in a noxious cocktail of scent and glass.

'Let's scram!' said Hughes. 'This place stinks.'

Another detonation threw eyeliner and blusher into the air, covering passers-by in black and red dye. Customers screamed and fled deeper into the store.

'Upstairs,' said Stafford.

Sean and Hughes waded through a sea of shoppers and reached a deserted escalator. It sat motionless, blocked by a chain barrier and a sign which read: 'Out of order'. Sean unclipped the barrier and scampered up the metal steps, trailed by Stafford and Hughes. Another blast struck a display stand and covered shoppers in shards of crockery.

'Control, we could use some help over here,' said Stafford into his neckpiece.

'Agent Stafford, your backup team is engaged in a fire-fight close to your current location.'

'Then tell them to get a move on!'

An energy bolt struck the escalator a few steps below him. It melted a hole the size of a beach ball into the escalator shaft. Stafford hurried up the last few steps and pulled out his sidearm.

'Hughes, get over here! We need to hold them off for as long as we can. Sean, see if you can find a fire escape.'

A few customers wandered around upstairs, uncertain whether to leave the store.

'This one's out of order; take the stairs,' said Stafford.

A boy noticed the weapon in Hughes' hand.

'I want one of those!'

'Trust me, kid, you really don't,' said Hughes. 'I'd run off home if I were you.'

'You can put it on your Santa List,' said his father, herding the boy towards the elevators.

For a few minutes, there was calm. Sean discovered a green fire exit sign a short distance away. On his way back, he discovered the sports department and selected a baseball bat, a skateboard and a tube of tennis balls. A shop assistant watched him rip open their packaging.

'And how are you going to pay for those, young man?'

'He'll pay,' said Sean, pointing at Stafford.

The assistant noticed Stafford's weapon and hurried away to find a superior.

Meanwhile, a dark grey figure appeared at the bottom of the escalator. It crouched and fired, melting part of the handrail. Stafford returned fire and struck the androbot's chest. It staggered back twitching, and a weapon fell from its hands.

'I need you to lie face down on the floor and spread out your arms!' cried a voice below.

It was a police officer armed with a Taser.

'Don't do it, officer! Run for your life!' cried Stafford.

The androbot raised an empty hand towards the policeman, who seemed puzzled by the gesture.

'This is your final warning. Lie face down on the floor or I'll fire!'

A bolt of blue energy swept from the androbot's wrist and struck the police officer in the midriff. As he fell, he unleashed the Taser. Its wires spiralled through the air and struck a mannequin dressed in a ladies outfit. Its plastic body sparked, and its wig caught fire. Meanwhile, the androbot recovered its weapon and limped out of sight.

****

Darius Deveraux watched a live video stream of the battle from his control room. An infrared camera followed three figures in an empty department store, and he grinned at what he saw.

'Order the androbots to take Yeager alive. Crush the other two; they are of no consequence.'

'Yes, master; it will be done,' said Seventy-one.

****

Without warning, the department store's lights went out. Hughes peered into the gloom.

'I can hear them coming.'

'You're not wrong,' said Stafford. 'Control, where's our nearest exit point?'

'Two hundred yards from your current location. Your phone app will guide you.'

Emergency lights came on, and Stafford spotted Sean crouched between two aisles, his arms full of sports equipment. Stafford crept nearer, and a volley of energy bolts struck the ceiling above him.

'Get out of here, Sean!' cried Stafford, diving for cover.

A dark figure blocked Sean's route to the fire exit. He hurled a tennis ball at its head, and the androbot fired. The tennis ball exploded in a cloud of yellow fluff. Stafford and Hughes moved from aisle to aisle, firing as they went. Around them, toys exploded on all sides. They were surrounded.

Sean rolled the skateboard towards the steady glow of the fire exit and stepped on board. He pushed frantically and readied the baseball bat. He had almost evaded the androbot's grasping hands when it stuck out a leg and sent him sprawling. A blast wave struck the creature, and it fell sideways, flattening a rack of sports shoes.

'Go, Sean! Go!' cried Stafford.

Sean reached the fire escape, smashed a glass cylinder and forced open a pair of heavy doors. A piercing alarm sounded, and Sean ran out into the daylight. He reached an empty stairwell and hurried down the first flight of steps. An androbot smashed through a window and landed on a lower landing. It wore a reflective visor and black body armour. It brushed broken glass from its overalls and stood watching him.

'Leave me alone; you freak!' said Sean, brandishing his baseball bat.

The androbot raised a hand and exposed a row of tubes in its wrist. It fired a volley of darts, but Sean dodged to one side, and they pinged against the concrete stairs. The androbot shook its head and extended a fingertip to reveal a sharp needle. It beckoned to him, and Sean panicked.

'Now what can I do? Watch, alive.'

The androbot flexed its legs and leapt up the stairs in a single bound. Sean swung his bat at the creature's chest, but the androbot wrenched it from his grasp and dropped it into the stairwell. Terrified, Sean ran back to the fire escape. More detonations sounded in the toy department, but there was no sign of Stafford or Hughes. The androbot lunged forwards and grabbed Sean's wrist. It raised its needle finger and prepared to stab him in the neck.

'Watch, protect me!' cried Sean.

His watch face span around and fired a flash of red light at the androbot's visor. The laser beam pierced a hole in the androbot's visor. It cradled its head in its hands and let out a scream. Sean's watch spoke.

'Get away from that thing, Sean! This is Captain Ayres; meet me at street level.'

Sean scurried down the stairs as fast as he could. A blaster bolt rang out behind him, and the androbot fell over the handrail.

'Hurry, Sean!' said Stafford, emerging from the shop.

'Where's Hughes?'

'Doing his job.'

At the bottom of the stairs, Sean crashed through another fire escape and ran outside. He was joined by Stafford.

'Exit Point, one hundred feet ahead,' said Stafford's phone.

'This way!'

Two androbot craft appeared at tree height and swooped down to attack. They fired a broadside of energy bolts and devastated a row of shop fronts. Sean hid behind a concrete pillar and waited, trembling.

'Sean! This way!'

Stafford waited beside a green, portable toilet and waved towards him.

'Over here! Run!'

'To a toilet?'

Before Sean could move, an androbot rammed its flying craft into a shop window between him and Stafford. The androbot staggered from the wreckage and raised its weapon. Stafford aimed his blaster and tried to fire, but nothing happened. In frustration, he threw it at the assailant. The androbot shrugged it off and fired at Stafford's feet.

'Run past it, Sean! You can do it!'

Sean watched the androbot with wary eyes. It aimed an arm and fired. Sean ducked, but he moved too soon. One dart skimmed his left arm and another struck his right. He staggered and fell on the pavement. Stafford ran from the toilet and lunged at the androbot. Before he could make contact, an energy bolt struck the creature's back, and it collapsed where it stood. Sean lay on the ground beside him.

Stafford came to lying in a puddle of white liquid. A gloved hand reached down and hauled him to his feet. It was Captain Ayres.

'Come on, Staffy. We need to get Sean to a medic.'

'Better late than never.'

'It was just a case of mind over matter. Come on, I need your help.'

They carried Sean to the portable toilet and rested him on a fake toilet seat.

'I'll never get used to these things,' said Stafford.

'Pleasant trip,' said Ayres, closing the door.

Stafford reached up to a hidden cover on the ceiling and slid it to one side. He punched in a code and pressed his thumb on a blue pad.

'Collection port active,' said a male voice. 'Awaiting rescue craft.'

An interior light flashed, and a blast of air pulled them skyward. Stafford passed out. Moments later, he found himself lying on the floor of a Hyperjet. Sean lay beside him, barely breathing.

'Medic!' cried Stafford, raising an arm.

'What have you done to him?' said a figure, kneeling beside him.

'Kept him alive, mostly,' said Stafford, rolling on his side and wincing. 'There's a dart in his arm.'

'Got it. Relax, we'll be at Kimbleton Hall in a couple of minutes.'

The medic gave Sean an injection and waved smelling salts

under his nose. He let out a groan.

'Sean? Can you hear me? Sean?'

Welcome to the world of Sean Yeager. Watch out! There are androbots and sleepers everywhere.

Sean Yeager Hunters Hunted is available in print now.